The Search

The Search

Tricia Haddon

T

The manufacturer's authorised representative in the EU
for product safety is Authorised Rep Compliance Ltd,
71 Lower Baggot Street, Dublin D02 P593 Ireland (www.arccompliance.com)

This is a work of fiction. Names, characters, businesses, places, events
and incidents are either the products of the author's imagination
or used in a fictitious manner. Any resemblance to actual persons,
living or dead, or actual events is purely coincidental.

Troubador Publishing Ltd
Unit E2 Airfield Business Park,
Harrison Road, Market Harborough,
Leicestershire. LE16 7UL
Tel: 0116 2792299
Email: books@troubador.co.uk
Web: www.troubador.co.uk

ISBN 978 1836281 566

British Library Cataloguing in Publication Data.
A catalogue record for this book is available from the British Library.

Printed and bound by CPI Group (UK) Ltd, Croydon, CR0 4YY
Typeset in 11pt Minion Pro by Troubador Publishing Ltd, Leicester, UK

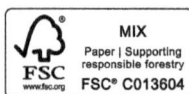

MIX
Paper | Supporting
responsible forestry
FSC® C013604

To
My sisters
Wendy (winks) and in memory of the late Margie for inspiration, encouragement and laughter.

The truth is rarely pure and never simple.
Oscar Wilde

If the phrase 'be careful what you wish for' had crossed Jenny's mind as she commenced her search, she may have thought twice about continuing and long-lost relatives would have remained lost.

Prologue

2007

Five words spoken twenty-six years ago had led to this.

'Thank you,' she whispered, 'thank you.' Barker the cocker spaniel in the cottage next door lived up to his name by seemingly echoing her gratitude.

'Shut up, shut up.' Her neighbour shouted his usual rebuke.

Jenny stared at the screen for several minutes, then stood up. She felt her legs weaken so gripped the front of her computer desk. She took six deep breaths in and then slowly out to calm herself while looking out of her bedroom window at the parish church across the road. She thought of Toby the mongrel dog they had years ago and whose ashes were scattered in the churchyard they had often strolled through on their walks. But this morning, being midday, there was nobody about. *I need a drink*, Jenny thought, moistening her dry lips with her tongue. She walked out of her bedroom to the top of the stairs, and, holding onto the banister – something that she hardly ever did – stepped carefully down each wooden step. She walked through the sitting room, which stretched the length of the cottage and into a side extension that contained the kitchen. Opening the fridge, she reached for a bottle of sparkling water. 'No, you idiot, not today,' she mumbled and pulled out a bottle of Chardonnay – which they were saving for a friend's party – instead. Picking up a wine glass from the worktop, she filled it to the top, walked across to the back door, sat down on the wooden bench in the tiny lobby, and stared into the garden at the holly tree, which gave their cottage its name and in winter was covered with berries. It stood against a crumbling brick wall that surrounded the narrow garden. She sipped her wine and wondered who she would tell first, then decided she didn't want to tell anyone. Not Lorna, who wouldn't be interested; not Nicky, who would; and not even Martin, who had supported her throughout her search – at least not yet. It was her discovery, and hers alone. She thought that this must be how Victorian plant hunters must have felt at the end of their lifetime quest for some exotic rare species as they knelt in front of their precious find in some remote corner of the globe, wanting to keep their discovery to themselves, for as long as possible. To share it would spoil the moment and the time when only they knew. A pleasure similar to sexual fulfilment.

Part One

1

1986

Hove Municipal Library was a honey-stone, double-fronted monument to Victorian self-improvement. A person only had to enter its black-and-white tiled vestibule, its walls covered with posters of local museums, adult classes and concerts, to feel enlightened. Jenny remembered how she had loved coming here as a child when, after choosing her reading quota of four books for three weeks, she would then climb the spiral stone stairway to the reference section where the travel books were kept. Black-and-white photos of exotic tribesmen from the Amazon to Zanzibar transported her to other worlds. Now, she was ready to begin her journey. It was the right time. Over the past three years, Martin and herself had settled into living together and adjusted to most, but not all, of their differences. They had recently moved from their two-bedroomed rented cottage in Falmer to Holly Cottage, a larger one with a second floor, bought with difficulty but helped by a joint mortgage. It stood in a terrace with nine others – their rendered walls painted in different pastel shades – in the ancient village of Patcham, just north of Brighton.

'Do you have copies of the local papers for 1945?' Jenny asked a middle-aged woman with glasses hanging on a cord around her neck, who was sitting perched behind a tall wooden desk at the top of the stairs.

'We do, we have the *Gazette*, *Evening Argus* and the *Brighton Weekly News*. But they're all on microfilm now.' The librarian pointed to rows of metal cabinets at the end of the room. 'They're in drawers in six-monthly boxes in year order, the oldest at the back. So, if you find the correct year and months for the paper you want, I'll find you a reader. Being Monday, we do have one free; usually you have to book by the hour.'

'I'm sorry, I didn't realise that.'

'You haven't used one before then.'

'No.'

'It's easy; I'll get you set up. Which paper do you want?'

Might be for you, Jenny thought, knowing from experience that when anyone said that, the task usually proved to be anything but. 'The *Weekly News*,' she said, thinking she could then cover more weeks in her time here. Minutes later, Jenny was scanning the *Brighton Weekly News* from January 1945 while trying to stop the page from shooting upwards whenever she touched the side lever. She was hoping that the reel wouldn't spin to the end when she would then have to ask the woman to set her up again. January, February and March slipped by.

After two hours, she was at the end of April 1945 and thinking that she would have to come back on another day when she wasn't working, when then, on the front page, a grainy black-and-white photo of a group of soldiers in

4

uniform appeared. 'Yes, yes,' she said out loud. A bald-headed man seated opposite looked up from his reader and adjusted his steel-framed glasses to see where the sound was coming from, then immediately looked back down with silent intent. The heading to the photo read, *The First South Africans arrive in Hove from POW camps in Eastern Europe for Rest and Recuperation.*

So, they were here, she thought, *the date is correct.*

Jenny continued reading the paper for the following weeks from May until August 1945. *I'll just have to be late home*, she thought. *I can't leave now.* Every week, there was an article about the South African soldiers. How they were recovering from their incarceration. What activities had been arranged for them while staying in Hove. Where they were travelling to if well enough to use their free rail passes. How local families had asked them to their homes for meals and invitations were handed out for local dances. They were billeted in requisitioned houses, radiating north from the seafront. Their headquarters and a canteen were based in a local school. By the end of July 1945, over ten thousand South African POWs were ready for repatriation.

*

'How's your day been then?' Jenny asked as Martin came into the kitchen, went straight over to the fridge, reached inside for a bottle and, snapping off the metal top with an opener, poured himself a lager.

'Busy. The new girl started today. It's always tiring showing a new person the ropes, but she's keen to learn,

5

so hopefully she'll stay longer than the last one. Are you going to join me?' He reached into a wooden cupboard for another glass, knowing her answer.

'What's her name?' Jenny glanced up at Martin from the kitchen chair, thinking how much he resembled Ricco, his Italian father, with his olive skin and dark hair.

'Isobel. But she prefers to be called Izzy.'

'Not dizzy Izzy I hope then. Will she be working with you?'

'Some of the time, but mostly she'll be in the office, for a while anyway. It's her first job since leaving uni.'

Jenny took her glass from Martin and started to sip her lager. She wondered if every woman who has left her marriage for another man felt as she did at the mention of another woman's name. *If someone has left once, they can do it again.* It was always the same reaction. Dread in the pit of her stomach while examining Martin's face for clues that she didn't want to see. She supposed, or rather hoped, that it must be the same for him when she mentioned a man's name from the office where she worked as a probate administrator. But he had more opportunity. A year ago, he had left his job with East Sussex County Council as a warden at the Seven Sister's Country Park and was now a warden with the Nature Conservancy Council, the national body for protecting National Nature Reserves and Sites of Special Scientific Interest. He was always out and about all over Sussex now, with no regular hours. He had never given her any solid reason to be jealous. But who needs a reason? He was devoted to his work, but how did that help? It made it worse. An adoring young assistant would be irresistible to anyone. He wouldn't even be aware of her attraction to him. A previous girl, Janine, had come and gone quite quickly without any explanation and now there was this Izzy. She would make time to visit his office on her next day off. She supposed this must be her punishment for leaving her marriage. She had planned on telling him what she had discovered at the library earlier, but the excitement had gone. She would tell him tomorrow.

2

To the editor,

Please would you be so kind as to place the following letter on the letters page of your newspaper:

I would very much like to hear from any South African ex-POW who was stationed at the Union Defence Force Repatriation Unit in Hove, East Sussex, England, during 1945. I would be interested to hear about their experiences during the last war, and also when they were staying at Hove awaiting repatriation.

All letters will be gratefully received and acknowledged.

Jenny had read, reread and then amended her short letter addressed to both the *Cape Times* and the *Johannesburg Star.* Finally, she was satisfied. Her last draft was brief and to the point but didn't give too much information away. She wanted the reader to be curious. She signed it *Jennifer Maynard* – her married name – sealed it in an envelope and dropped it in her bag to be posted at the main post office during her lunch break.

'Sorry, can't stop today, Mr Wainwright,' Jenny shouted out of her car window at her elderly neighbour who, on seeing her drive up Church Hill, had stopped mowing the grass banks in front of the church and started walking towards the road. She parked in her usual place opposite their cottage and, not bothering to lock her car, ran over to the front door fumbling in her bag as she stood on the top step for her key. As she pushed the door open, a pile of blue airmail letters that she had seen on leaving for work that morning – but had not had time to open – lay scrunched up on the doormat. Jenny scooped them up and ran into the kitchen. Choosing a sharp knife from the terracotta jar on the worktop, she sat down at the table and sliced open the first letter.

Dear Jennifer,

I was intrigued to know why you placed your letter in the Cape Times. *I always take this paper but have never seen a letter before from someone in England asking why we South Africans were in Hove in 1945…*

Jenny opened the second letter, and almost word for word, the writer asked the same question. She opened and scanned all eleven airmails, each one saying they had never before seen a letter from someone in England asking about them and were interested to know why she had written the letter. Her careful wording had worked. She sighed and relaxed back into her chair, bent down and took a copy of her original letter from her bag, smiling as she reminded herself of what she had written. She stood up and, reaching for a half-full bottle of Rioja that stood next to the gas hob, poured herself a glass, sat back down and started to read the pile of airmail letters again – this time more thoroughly.

'Jenn, what are those?' The question came from behind her.

'For God's sake, you made me jump. I didn't hear you come in.' She turned and smiled at Martin as he filled the doorway.

'Sorry, I didn't mean to. But I was standing here and you were miles away.'

'Yes, I was, literally. Do you remember I said I was going to write to the South African newspapers?'

'I thought you had changed your mind. That was a while ago.'

'Well, I did write, eventually. I just wanted to be sure that the wording was right. I didn't want to put anyone off from replying. I can't believe it, but I've had eleven replies today.'

'Wow, I see you're celebrating by finishing off the Rioja. I'll get myself a glass and join you. I must say, we seem to be making a habit lately of drinking before our meal. I'm thinking perhaps we ought to cut down a bit, say, no more than twice a week. Can you remind me if I forget that I've got to call Richard before eight about the arrangements for putting the ponies on Lullington Heath for grazing tomorrow? They do a fantastic job at keeping the scrub down.'

'I did enjoy our walk up there last Saturday. So many butterflies, and ones I've never seen before too. I never knew that heathland could exist on the top of the Downs.' Their shared love of the countryside added to their physical attraction and ensured that they were never short of conversation.

'Are you going to reply to all of those, then?' He filled

his glass with what remained in the bottle and joined her at the table.

'Yes, definitely. I can't leave them wondering why I wrote my letter, can I? They've made the effort to write and tell me about their experiences.'

'Do you think one might be from your birth father?' He ran his fingers through a lock of hair that always flopped over his forehead.

'That would be too much to ask. Did you know there were nearly ten thousand South African POWs living here in Sussex in 1945? I had no idea there were so many. I can hardly write and ask them about their sex life while they were here, can I? Also, any possible father is unlikely to reply to my letter after all this time, even if they can remember they could be. I need to know more about how they came to be in Hove. Everyone knows about the Americans and Canadians being over here, but no one has ever mentioned the South Africans. Well, I have never heard of them being here anyway. Some have English names, some Afrikaans names and some Jewish names, so they were a mixture.'

'Probably because they were taken prisoner in North Africa and weren't part of the liberation of Europe like the others. Not such a feel-good story being captured by the enemy, is it?' He stood up and, leaning over, wrapped his arms around her in a bear hug and planted a kiss on the top of her head, saying, 'Well done, Jenny.'

She turned, tilting her head back so her lips pressed against his.

He ran his hands through her dark hair and then slid them inside her blouse and under her bra, cupping and massaging her breasts until her nipples hardened. 'Mm this feels good.'

'So will this, Martin Barretti.' Jenny stood up and, whispering into his ear, said, 'Guess what? I've drunk too much wine on an empty stomach and Lorna's not coming back 'til later. Are you going to take advantage of me then?' She grinned as she unbuckled his belt and loosened his jeans, then slid her hand inside his boxer shorts.

'It certainly does, Jenn. Too good. But I think it's the other way round, don't you? But I'm not raising any objections,' he whispered. 'I take back what I said about us not having a drink before dinner, we should do it more often, not less.' He placed his hand over hers. 'Stop for a moment or I'll come. We can do better than this.' He dropped his shorts and trousers, releasing his erection.

'We certainly can.' Jenny stepped out of her underwear and, gathering her skirt up around her waist, she pulled him towards her and covered his mouth with her own. Martin pushed her back against the worktop and, breathing heavily, massaged her slowly until his fingers were wet and, glancing across at the clock on the wall, whispered, 'Oh shit, too late to phone Chris now, in more ways than one.'

'Now, now.' Jenny moaned.

'Quick, quick.' He panted as he grabbed her legs; pulling them up and wrapping them around his body, he thrust into her.

*

Over the next month, thirty-one more airmail letters from POWs fell through the letterbox. Each one, with a

12

slight deviation, told of how they were young volunteers with the South African Defence Force in 1940 and eager to fight Rommel's Germans in the desert of North Africa. How they were captured, first by the Italians, experiencing terrible conditions in the searing heat while waiting to be taken to Italy. Then, dodging Allied torpedoes – some of which hit their target – they were shipped to Italian prisoner-of-war camps, then later transferred by the Germans to camps in Eastern Europe in which to spend the rest of the war. There were harrowing descriptions of death marches westward with their captors in the freezing winter of 1945 – accompanied by concentration camp survivors – to escape the advancing Red Army. Once those that had survived reached the Allies, they were fed and rested, although some then died from eating too much too soon in their malnourished state. They were then transported to Hove for a period of rest and recuperation from their ordeal, before eventual repatriation by ship to South Africa.

3

1988

'Why can't you go in search of your birth mother, Jenny? You said you wanted to a couple of years ago when we were living at Falmer. I remember you telling me then that the law had changed and you could find information about your birth family if you wanted to. You must remember? Didn't you make an appointment with someone, a social worker? Then, I think you cancelled it because you felt ill or you needed more time or something. I can't quite remember the reason. Well, you've had more time, so why not do it now? Make another appointment; from what you told me, it would be a lot easier, and cheaper.' Martin grinned. 'At least she's English and she's probably still alive. Her name would be in your adoption file, wouldn't it? Also, more importantly, your father's name could be there too.'

'Mum told me she was just a young local girl. My father sounds much more interesting.'

'What's interesting got to do with it? She's your birth mother, and if you traced her, she should be able to give you a name, at least the Christian name, of your father. I

14

can't understand why you don't want to find her? You'll never trace him without a name.'

Jenny felt her cheeks reddening so turned away to avoid looking at Martin. 'I know it sounds shallow, saying he sounds more interesting than my mother. But it's not just about tracing him or even meeting him. He's a part of me. I just want to know all about him and perhaps even go to South Africa while we have the chance. We can go, Martin. We have some savings. It just takes a bit of planning.'

Once Jenny had replied to all the letters she had received, explaining her interest – but trying not to put any of them off by mentioning that she was searching for her father – correspondence with half a dozen, who were keen to elaborate on their experiences, continued regularly. One man wrote once a month, with a full serialised account – enough to fill the pages of a book – of his time from 1940 to 1945 and beyond. She learnt from their letters that South Africans who volunteered later during the war were involved in the liberation of Europe. They had joined up with other allied armies, fighting their way up from the foot of Italy to Germany. Offers were made to Jenny, if they were able to visit at some time in the future, to show them around, stay in their homes and even provided names and information on suitable local hotels.

'I don't know about actually going there, Jenn. I'm still supporting Daniel. We have Lorna living here. Then there's Nicky. We don't have any spare money. Perhaps in a year or two.'

Jenny thought, not for the first time, they would have more money if Marilyn – his now ex-wife – put herself out to do more paid work, rather than spend so much of her time going to the gym and socialising. But she knew Martin would never say anything to her. He always made some excuse when she mentioned the subject – usually involving Daniel – as to why she couldn't work more hours. *Leaver's guilt*, she thought, but now was not the time to bring it up.

'I can use my bonus money. We've had a busy year, lots of winter flu, that always means more clients. Lorna and Nicholas always stay with Rob in the February half-term, which would be a good time weather-wise to go, so a few extra days wouldn't hurt them, although I know Rob will plead work commitments. Daniel can stay with Marilyn or a friend; he'll only miss one weekend here. Tell Marilyn it's really important. Not that she'll think it is. We have all these offers to show us around and to stay, which means we don't have to spend money on hotels if we don't want to. We may never get another chance.'

'Sounds to me as though you've got it all worked out.'

4

Maureen looked across at Jenny with her sad eyes as she sat hunched in the armchair under the sash window in Jenny's sitting room. 'I'm so pleased I can come to these meetings. They really help me. No one understands my loss except other birth mothers. Everyone else that I know, especially my family, expect me to forget that I ever gave birth and get on with my life. But a part of me is missing and always will be unless I find her.'

'Well, I wish more would come along to these meetings, but I think they're under the impression they are only for adoptees.' For the past six months, Jenny had been a local contact leader for NORCAP, an organisation to help adoptees trace their birth families and give support. Birth mothers and adoptive parents were welcome, but adoptees always outnumbered everyone else. Since 1975, adult adoptees had been able to access their original birth records after the required meeting with a social worker who would support the adoptee and mention some of the ramifications of being told the information. Some were content just to have names of their birth mothers and reasons for their adoption, while others placed their names on NORCAP's contact list so they could be found by any birth relative who also placed their name on the register. Once they were matched up, an intermediary would write a carefully worded letter – so as not to arouse suspicion about an adoption if a third party read it – to the birth mother, to see what contact she would be willing to have. Only an intermediary could access both records. This had been decided on as the most appropriate way of bringing the child and usually the birth mother together.

Some adoptees only wanted information, while others wanted to meet. Jenny knew of no mother – after recovering from the shock of receiving a letter from the intermediary – who refused to know anything about their child. So even if the mother couldn't face a reunion, they were nearly all willing to either write a letter or provide more information. Some adoptees, once they knew their birth mother's name, undertook their own research, and Jenny, if asked, would help if the family were local by checking old street directories and newspapers. If she was successful, she then advised the adoptee to use an intermediary to make the initial contact. Birth mothers – not being allowed to access their child's adoption records – could only wait until their child made the first contact. Jenny held her meetings once every three months, nearly always on the evenings when Martin was out tutoring an evening class on nature conservation.

'It really helps me cope,' continued Maureen. 'Just to know how adoptees feel about their birth mothers. I feel so guilty all the time, I'm always thinking that my daughter – Sarah, I called her – will never want to know me because I gave her up, but I had no choice.' Jenny knew her story. She had been working as a Red Coat at a Butlin's holiday camp when she found herself pregnant by her boyfriend, another Red Coat. When the season ended and she returned home, her father, along with her boyfriend, wanted nothing more to do with her or her unborn child, so, as was usual, she had been sent to a local mother-and-baby home run by the church. She was now in her forties and had no other children, so her life was dominated by needing to have information about her child, and unless her daughter made contact via the registers, she had no hope of obtaining any. Guilt was the main emotion felt by all the birth mothers. Although all the adoptees that Jenny knew had no ill feelings towards them, assuming correctly that without family support, their mothers had no choice but to place them for adoption by a married couple, who could give their child a better life than they could offer at that time.

'How's your own search going, Jenny?' Maureen would ask at each meeting.

'Oh, I've given up trying to trace my birth mother,' Jenny would say. 'With a name like Annie Johnston, it's just too difficult. Too many spelling variations to check all the marriage and death registers. It would take me years and cost a fortune to buy all the certificates I would need to check I had the right person. So, I'm searching for my birth father instead.'

'But didn't you say he's South African?' added Briony, a blonde, even-featured woman, whose birth mother had been a ballet dancer made pregnant by an older, married choreographer, who promptly abandoned her. 'That's going to be difficult too.'

'Yes, it is, but we're planning on going to South Africa in a year or two when Lorna and Nicky have finished studying, so I'm hoping that I'll be able to find out more information there.'

5

1989

The letter from Germany was just another reply to add to her collection. Like agents' rejection letters that successful authors keep as trophies of their belief in their work and their persistence, Jenny needed to keep them. She wondered why she still bothered to keep searching when she knew what any replies would say. But, although she had told Martin she would stop searching, she was compelled to pursue all possible links, no matter how tenuous.

As I'm sure you are aware, during the war and the difficult times afterward, huge gaps appeared in all military records. A lot of material was destroyed in compliance with instructions. Personal documents regarding POWs were kept by the Office of the Wehrmacht in Meiningen. Soviet troops moved here in July 1945 and records were taken to an unknown destination. Unfortunately, the Soviet Archives do not know where the documents might be.

With friendly greetings,
Herr Stadler

Jenny sighed as she read the English translation of the letter from the Military Archives at Freiburg. She had hoped that German efficiency would help in her search, having discovered that photos of every prisoner had been taken on their arrival at their final designated camp in German-occupied Europe and attached to their camp record. *The records are in Russia*, she thought, *that's impossible*. She had hoped that if they were still in Germany, she might have been able to visit and search the records, putting to the back of her mind again that she had no name to search for.

She decided not to tell Martin of this latest non-development. There was no point; she knew what his reaction would be. He would say again how easier it would be if she traced her birth mother and she would again be reminded of what she wanted and needed to forget. Before writing to Germany, she had written to the international headquarters of the Red Cross in Geneva, where all POW records dating back to 1863 – when the organisation was incorporated – were kept. A quick reply informed her that without a person's name, they too were regretfully unable to locate any record.

The front door slammed and Lorna, now at the local sixth form college, burst into the kitchen, throwing her bag onto the floor and grabbing an apple from the fruit bowl on the worktop.

'Guess what Hannah said to me today? I'll kill that fucking cow.'

'Don't talk like that, Lorna.' Jenny was jolted from thinking about her latest letter by the arrival of her daughter with puffy eyes and mascara tracks running down her cheeks.

'She's only going out with Liam. She knows I've fancied him for ages. She's such a bitch.' Lorna picked up Jenny's letter, glanced at it, and threw it back on the table.

'It might not be true. She may just be saying that to wind you up.'

'Don't be so ridiculous. What do you know about it at your age anyway?' Lorna bit into the apple and, tossing her long hair over her shoulders, ran out of the room shouting, 'Don't speak to me.' Jenny heard her thunder up the stairs, and then the walls of the cottage shook as she slammed her bedroom door behind her.

Jenny moved Lorna's bag from the middle of the kitchen floor into the lobby. She picked up the letter from Germany and slid it inside a folder to join the many others, wondering, not for the first time, why children always think that their parents are ignorant about their strong feelings. She decided that children don't like to think of them as having any, as that would then detract from their own. It's the same as thinking that their parents never have sex, despite the evidence to the contrary. Especially as, in her own case, she had left Lorna's father for Martin. Most of the time – she lived with them during the week and with Rob alternate weekends – Lorna seemed indifferent to Martin, but whenever she caught them kissing – which was seldom as they tried not to antagonise her – she would quickly leave the room muttering, 'Ugh, how gross.'

Jenny recalled Martin's words the other night as they lay side by side in bed after making love.

'Jenn, we could still try for a baby, you know. It's not too late. You're still having regular periods. Daniel will be off my hands financially soon. We would love our own child so much; well, I would anyway, especially if it was a girl, like her mother.'

Jenny dreaded him mentioning the subject, which he did from time to time since they had moved into their current cottage. She knew he wanted another child, only having Daniel. So, she replied, 'I know you would love our baby, and hopefully I would too, although I'm not an earth-mother type. I love you, Martin, but I just don't think I can have another baby, not at my age. What about the risks? I would be a geriatric mother. Broken nights, nappies, potty training, starting everything over again. I love my job and I'm hoping to be a manager there soon. Then there are our mortgage payments; we need my salary. Even if I kept my job, who would look after the baby when I went back to work? There's only Ricco, and he's elderly and unwell. I will think about it, though, perhaps we could work something out.'

'Thank you, Jenn,' he said as he turned and kissed her on the lips.

6

'Jennifer, Jennifer Maynard?' A young woman with a mass of red hair stood on the front step, the bright morning sun making her hair appear like a halo of fire.

'Yes, that's me, come inside.'

'I'm Andrea Knight from the *Evening Argus*. Shall I call you Jennifer or Jenny?'

'Jenny's fine.' She smiled as she ushered the woman through the door and beckoned for her to sit down in an armchair.

'When you contacted us, I was intrigued to find out more about you and your story. So perhaps we can help you in some way.'

'I hope so. I'll make us a drink first. Tea or coffee?'

'Coffee, definitely, Jenny. This is a lovely position for a cottage, so cosy inside too.'

Five minutes later, as Jenny settled into her armchair opposite the reporter, Andrea said, 'I probably should have mentioned this on the phone, but I have Steve, our photographer, in the car outside, so would it be alright if we take a photo of you? There's always more interest shown in a story if we can add a picture of the person involved.'

'Oh, OK, uhm, just let me straighten my hair in the mirror first.'

'Sorry, I should have asked you before. I'll call him in and we can get that bit over with.' Ten minutes later, as Steve closed the front door behind him, Andrea reached into her bag for a notebook and pen and said with a smile, 'Well, we'll make a start, shall we? Some of my colleagues now use hand-held recorders, they're useful for outdoor interviews, but I still prefer to make handwritten notes as I find I get a better feel for the story from watching the person, listening and making notes. So, Jenny, tell me a bit about yourself first and then about your search.'

*

'Wow, that's a really interesting story. I have a few questions for you though. How did it make you feel when you discovered that you had been adopted?'

'Well, obviously I was shocked, very shocked. I had no idea, and sixteen is a difficult age anyway.'

'Yes, it is. But did it make you hate your adoptive parents for not telling you earlier?'

'No, of course not, they were lovely people. The shock made me ill though. I suffered from anxiety – agoraphobia – for several years. I even spent a short time in hospital.'

'I didn't know people were kept in hospital for that sort of thing. That must have been very difficult for you.'

'It was a hospital for nervous disorders and depression; it doesn't exist anymore. You could attend as a day patient or, if necessary, as an in-patient. So no, not a good time, but I realise now I have children of my own that it's not always easy to tell someone you love what they should know. It's a bit like plucking up the courage to tell your children the facts of life; it's easier to keep putting it off because you know they might be upset and embarrassed, and you know that you will be too.'

'Yes, I see,' she said, biting the end of her pen. But it was plain to Jenny that she didn't. 'Anyway, Jenny, how do you think we can help you in your search?'

'I know that without a name you can't help me find my father, but some of your readers must remember the South Africans being here at the end of the war, so they may be able to relate stories about them or remember what it was like with them here. That's what I would love to hear about.'

*

In the days following her interview, Jenny scanned the newspaper stands for her article. Then, a week later, on page three, there was a photo of herself staring back at her. Rushing home, she found Martin at the kitchen table reading an article from the local wildlife trust magazine. Waving the paper in front of him, she said, 'Martin, look at this. It's dreadful. Not only is there an awful, unflattering photo of me, and they've put my age in as well, but look at the headline and what she's written.'

Martin grabbed the paper from her and read, 'Divorced mother of two seeks information about her father. That's alright, isn't it?'

'But read the article, it makes me seem like some neurotic, ungrateful daughter seeking some unknown

27

soldier who seduced a young local girl, made her pregnant and then left the country.'

'Well, he did, didn't he? Journalists always make a story sound as dramatic as possible. It's what they do to sell their papers, and for some reason they always put people's ages in; I don't know why, but they always do. She must have asked you about your birth mother then?'

'Yes, she did, so I just told her what I told you.'

'But it does say at the end of the article for people to write in with their memories of that time. To be honest, I don't know why you contacted the newspaper in the first place. You already have all those letters from the POWs, so there can't be much more to add.'

'Well, we'll see. I just hope no one at work sees this.'

'Well, I wouldn't worry. If the photo is as bad as you think it is, they probably won't recognise you.' He grinned as he handed Jenny the newspaper.

7

1991

'This is ridiculous, Jenny. How can you possibly look through ten thousand record cards? We're only here for two days before we go to the game park. As I've said many times before, I want to support you, but it's impossible to find him without a name. You'll only be disappointed yet again.'

'Logically, I know it's impossible, but I need to see those cards. I even have a letter of introduction. It wasn't easy getting permission, I had to write to the South African Defence Force office, and then I waited ages for their reply,' Jenny said on the morning of their second day in South Africa.

'You kept that quiet, didn't you? Well, go if you must. I can see you're not going to be satisfied until you do. But I'm going to the Natural History Museum. I was hoping we could go together. They have a stuffed quagga on display. It's a chance in a lifetime to see what one looked like. I've only ever seen drawings of one up to now. Not quite the same as a live one, but I think I'm two hundred years too late. There used to be thousands of them roaming the veld around here two centuries ago, the same as the herds of bison in North America.' His eyes twinkled as he adjusted his khaki sun hat. 'Well, I suppose I'll meet you back here around six then. We could have a swim before dinner, to make the most of staying here.'

'I'll be back before then. So, yes, definitely a swim. Have you noticed how suddenly it gets dark here?'

'Yes, that's because we're nearer the equator. Take care. Don't get lost. I don't fancy wandering the streets looking for you in this heat.'

They were staying in Pretoria, at the Holiday Inn on Andries Street, opposite Burgers Park. The day before, they had taken afternoon tea in the park's café and watched as children of all colours intermingled in the playground. Apartheid was gradually being dismantled since FW De Klerk had been elected President of the National Party in late 1989, and a year ago, Nelson Mandela had walked free from Victor Verster Prison.

Clutching her letter, Jenny was ushered into a small, square room on the first floor of the Defence Force Archive building on Visagie Street. It was dusty, with two steel radiators under the window. *A replica of my 1950s classroom*, she thought, *only with bars across the window instead of Venetian blinds*. Against the three inner walls stood row upon row of long, thin, metal boxes, piled one on top of the other. The top one at head height. She stared at them, taking in the reality of being there. *My birth father's details are somewhere in this room*, she thought. Walking along the rows, she reached the letter 'M' and pulled out the drawer marked 'MO–MY'. Flicking through the index cards, she slowed when she reached the name

Myburgh. There was an Alan, two Fredriks, a Johannes, and then Louis Myburgh, the name of one of the POWs she was corresponding with. *So*, she thought, *the system works.* The cards were tightly packed together. With a tug, she pulled the card free from between its neighbours and read his address, next of kin, date of birth, regiment and number, but there was no description of him and no photograph. Keeping the card in her hand, she sat on the stone floor, staring at the boxes. She took the banana that she had saved from the breakfast buffet from her bag, peeled and ate it. *So*, she thought, *it looks like they are all here, but from the dust everywhere, they couldn't have been touched for decades. My father's card is in here somewhere, but where? Martin's right, it's impossible without a name, and anyway, there are no physical descriptions or photographs that I was hoping to see.* She sighed; she wasn't upset, just accepting of the reality that she had known all along. Putting the banana peel in her bag, she stood up and walked over to the window and peered out. People of various races were busy enjoying their lunch break. A newspaper vendor on the pavement opposite was standing by the entrance to a bank shouting the day's news. A heavily built man in khaki shorts bought a paper and then went inside. Two white women in floral summer dresses were walking along the pavement chatting and laughing as they passed the vendor. She watched for a further few minutes, then squeezed Louis Myburgh's card back in between his compatriots, picked up her bag and left the room, thinking that she would surprise Martin by joining him at the museum and seeing this quagga.

*

'I can't face sorting my case out now so I'm going to leave it here until tomorrow. I'll go and put the kettle on for some tea. I knew I would love South Africa, Martin, but you enjoyed it too, didn't you? Even though I knew you weren't keen on going,' said Jenny, putting her case by the downstairs cloakroom and walking into the kitchen.

'Of course I did, it was an amazing experience. Those marauding baboons on the way to Cape Point. I thought they were going to break the car aerial on Jack's car when they jumped on the bonnet. They're so much bigger and scarier in real life, like the lions in the game park.' Apart from visiting Pretoria, they had flown down to Cape Town to stay with Jack Sellick – one of Jenny's original correspondents – and his wife Joy. They lived in a flat off Kloof Nek Road under Table Mountain. True to his promise, as well as giving them a city tour and visiting Cape Point, he had driven them to Stellenbosch for wine tasting and then down to a windy Bloubergstrand for the obligatory photo of Table Mountain with the Atlantic surf in the foreground.

'I loved seeing those tortoises on the side of the road when we hired the car. They looked so strange ambling along. We only ever see them as pets here.'

'A bit more of a worry than hedgehogs if they decide to cross the road. More of a crunch too,' Martin said, laughing as Jenny gathered two mugs from their hooks.

'Oh no, don't say that. I preferred the Karoo to the Winelands. Those gravel roads go for miles. Jack thought we were mad, hiring a car and driving to Clanwilliam. He and Joy kept saying there was nothing there, but that's why I liked it. Everyone was so welcoming. That evening, when Lew and his wife came over to join us for dinner. They were hilarious, and so pleased to meet us and tell us all about his experiences during the war. But you know the other best thing?'

'No, surprise me; anyway, you can't have more than one best thing. Grammatically incorrect.'

'I've now visited both South African capital cities. I never knew there were two. Cape Town, their summer seat of government, and Pretoria, during their winter.' In that moment, as she waited for the kettle to boil, Jenny returned to her childhood when she thought she must be the only child who knew the names of all the capital cities in the world, and how she longed to visit them. Every evening when her father came home from work, he would relax in his armchair by the radio and she would undo the laces on his shoes, and if it was winter, replace them with warm slippers. He would then fire the name of a country at her, and she would reply with its capital.

Martin stood up from the table, grabbed Jenny's hand and pulled her towards him. 'Let's leave the teas and go upstairs before we fall asleep. Make the most of an empty house before Lorna comes home.'

'How can I resist an offer like that?' Jenny smiled. 'Especially from you.'

'Only from me, I hope.'

Jenny wondered why she could never say no to him, no matter when it was or wherever they were, not that he was especially demanding. Sexually, they were well matched and their physical attraction was still as strong as it had been eight years previously when they had accidently met each other again, twenty years after they first went out together as teenagers. He was a good-looking man with a tall, slender frame, but broad-shouldered. It had been all too easy to say no to Rob. She supposed that was what made her leaving him inevitable.

'Don't answer that. Let it ring,' Martin said, removing his trousers.

Jenny, now naked, reached across the bed for her dressing gown. 'It's probably Rob. Bad timing as usual, but I'd better go. I'll be quick. Can you put the fire on? It's cold up here.'

'Just let it ring then, for God's sake. He'll ring again if it's urgent. But it probably isn't, knowing Rob.' But Jenny had already left the bedroom. 'Why can't women ever leave a ringing phone?' Martin muttered as he clambered onto the bed. 'Hurry up,' he shouted.

'I thought it might be you. Is everything OK?' Jenny stood by the window cradling the phone in her hand. 'What do you mean, Rob, yes and no?' Jenny sat down on the chair beside the small table, her heart moving up a gear. 'OK, so he's been suspended, but surely he can go back on Monday?' Starting to shiver, she pulled her dressing gown across her body. 'Look, I can't deal with this at the moment. The plane was delayed, so we've only been back fifteen minutes. I'll call you tomorrow and come over at the weekend.' Jenny slammed the receiver down and stared out of the window. She sighed, pulled the telephone plug from the wall, and went back upstairs.

Martin was lying on the bed naked from the waist down. 'I told you to leave it. What's up? No, on second thoughts, don't tell me, look.' He pointed to his now-flaccid penis.

'I won't, don't worry.' Jenny flung herself down on the bed beside him, then, opening her dressing gown, she rolled on top of him. Parting her legs, she knelt over him and, bending forwards so he could fondle her breasts, she muttered, 'I need this first anyway. You'll be hard again in a minute. I'll make sure of that.'

*

'That was the best finale we could have to our trip, wasn't it?' Martin sighed as he lay back on the pillow, his hands behind his head.

'There wasn't much time for it in South Africa, was there? Trying to fit everything in, excuse the pun.' Jenny giggled as she reached for the box of tissues on the bedside table. 'Do you want one?'

'No, I'll take a shower in a minute. Then I'll have to get some sleep. I've work tomorrow. What I want now is a cigarette. I really miss it at times like this. Post-coital is the very best smoke you can have.'

Jenny wiped herself and threw the tissue in the basket. 'I'm sorry, I know you gave it up for me, and I really appreciate that. I'll go and make us that tea now instead; a poor substitute, I know.'

'Jenn, I want to say sorry. I know I wasn't as encouraging as I should have been on our trip. You did all that research and arranged everything, and all I could do was throw cold water on it.'

'No, I agree, you weren't encouraging. But you were

35

right. It's hopeless without a name. I'll have to give up searching. I know I've said this before, but I mean it this time. Do you want any tea?' She sat up and looked across, but he had already turned onto his side and all she could see was his dark hair on the pillow. He was snoring softly.

8

'Oh, aren't you sweet.' Jenny bent down to pat the grey French Bulldog that had bounded over to her as she wandered along Hove seafront.

A plump woman with short, dark, spiky hair was rushing towards her. 'Sadie, come here. I'm so sorry, she's only young.'

'That's OK, she's cute. Oh my God, Gail, it's you. I can't believe it. It's been ages since we've seen each other. Must be almost ten years.'

'Yes, where on earth have you been, Jenny? As you say, nearly ten years. I often think about you. I tried phoning you and I even called at your house, but the people there said they didn't know where you had moved to. Why haven't you contacted me?'

'I know, I should have. I'm really sorry.'

'Yes, you should have. I take it you did leave Rob for what's his name – was it Martin – Martin Barretti?'

'Yes, it is, and I did leave Rob, and he put our house up for sale. He lives near Guildford now. He married again as soon as our divorce was finalised; she's called Louise, I think he met her at work.'

'I remember the last time we met; you were unsure about leaving Rob because of Lorna and Nicky.'

Jenny remembered the last time she had seen Gail. She had bumped into her then too. It had been in the main shopping centre in Hove, and she had just emerged from visiting a travel agent.

'Yes, I was unsure. It was such a big step, but it was inevitable, and it hasn't been easy. There's always a price to pay, I suppose. But we're very happy together; we're not married, no plans to either. We bought a cottage in Patcham a couple of years ago. When we first lived together, we rented a cottage in Falmer. But, that's nothing to do with why I haven't contacted you for so long. I owe you an explanation. I don't think you knew I was adopted, did you?'

Gail bent down to put Sadie on a lead. 'No, I'm sure I would have remembered if you had told me. But what's that got to do with you not contacting me?'

'Well, I didn't find out about my adoption until I was sixteen. That's when you fell pregnant and had all your difficulties with Chris.'

'That bastard, don't remind me. It was such a terrible time. Although, I realised after I left him that he had a gambling addiction. Nothing else mattered to him, not even our children, only the next bet. I only had myself to blame though; I was an idiot. He was six years older than me and I thought he was so much more mature than the teenagers we knew. We should never have married.'

'No, you weren't. I remember how excited you were when you told me about him. It could have happened to any girl at that time, no pill back then, remember? We had to rely on the boy using a Durex or, as they say, "being careful". We all wanted to know what sex was like, didn't we? The first time's usually a disappointment anyway.'

'Well, it certainly was for me. It was over before I even knew it had begun. I still fell pregnant though.'

'At least girls don't have to get married now. Well, I was busy with my first job at that time and going out meeting boys. It didn't seem that important, although it was a terrible shock when I discovered that I had been adopted, it made me ill, and to be honest, I was too embarrassed and ashamed to tell anyone. I don't know why I felt so ashamed, but I did. So, I only told Rob after we'd been going out for a while because I was so worried he wouldn't want to see me again. He was the only person I did tell until I met Martin again. Look, we can't talk here, not after all these years. Let's go to Matteo's, remember their ice creams? We were always going there when we were teenagers. I'll treat you and explain. I owe you that at least.'

They walked side by side towards Brighton. Jenny pointed to the multicoloured beach huts – most were painted in a pastel shade, but a few had two-colour stripes – that lined the promenade. 'They must be newly painted, surely? I don't remember them looking as pristine as that the last time I was down here. You look just the same though, Gail. I would recognise you anywhere,' Jenny said, noticing a few grey hairs in her friend's spikes and her gold, hooped earrings.

'Yes, the whole prom has been smartened up quite recently. It did look really neglected for a few years. Glad you think I look much the same. I don't always feel it though.'

After deciding what flavours to choose, they sat outside the parlour on plastic chairs and looked out at the slate-grey sea. Jenny wondered why on earth she hadn't contacted her friend for so long. It was the same with Dido, her old work colleague who now lived – or did, the last time she had heard – in America. 'Are you still teaching, Gail?'

'Not full-time now, thank goodness, that's why we bought Sadie. I love teaching but it's not easy these days. It's so hard controlling the children. We're so limited in what we can do to discipline them. There's no respect anymore, even with the little ones. I've even had some swear at me. It's not how it was in our schooldays. These ice creams are fantastic, by the way.' She bent down to offer the expectant Sadie a lick from her cone.

'Yes, they're the best, there are always queues here. That's awful, Gail. I remember the most we dared to do was to be cheeky. Do you remember Susan Chandler? She answered back once and was sent to the headmistress. We thought that was terrible. I never even knew four-letter words existed, or what they meant, until I was in my twenties.'

'Well, they certainly know them all now before they go up to secondary school. Come on, you still haven't explained why you haven't contacted me.'

'Well, once Martin and I were settled, I decided to search for my birth parents.'

'Who, your birth mother?'

'No, she died.'

'Oh, I'm sorry, Jenny.'

'No, that's alright, thank you though. So, no, my birth father. He was, or is, South African, so it's not easy, especially as I don't have a name, and it's taking up all my spare time. I'm trying every avenue I can think of, writing here, there and everywhere. I even contacted the *Evening Argus* a couple of years ago, not that there was much response, just a couple of letters. You didn't see the article then?'

Gail stopped licking her ice cream. 'No, I didn't. What, you don't have a name? How can you find him then? That's crazy. You mean there's nothing on your birth certificate then?'

'Not on my original birth certificate – I also have an adoption certificate – no, there's just a blank. If the father didn't attend the registration, his name wasn't entered on the birth certificate. Mum told me just before she died that he was a soldier from South Africa, and I was to try and find him, so that's all the information I know. In fact, we've just come back from South Africa. So, I suppose that's the closest I'll ever get to him.'

'That's amazing, Jenny. I've always wanted to go there. Well, you certainly look very happy so perhaps finding him is not that important. Anyway, suppose you do trace him, what will you do if he denies being your father? He could, couldn't he? It could all be for nothing.' She bent down to let Sadie have another lick of her ice cream, which was quickly disintegrating onto the pavement.

'No, you're right, he could deny it and might not want anything to do with me. But, if that does happen, I'll just have to be satisfied with having some information about him, that's what's important to me, the information. I probably wouldn't want to actually contact him in person. Unfortunately, though, this search has become a bit of an obsession; that's what Martin thinks, and he keeps telling me so. I'm always thinking about what else I can do. I just can't let it go. I also volunteer for NORCAP, it's a charity that helps other adoptees to trace their birth relatives. So, although none of this is an excuse, at least you know the reason why I've been so busy and not kept in touch. Tell me, did you ever become a councillor?'

'Yes, I did, and I still represent Wish Ward. It was me that pressed the council to update Hove promenade. So, I see the result of my work every time I walk Sadie. I've even been thinking about standing as MP for Hove; Labour, of course. Gerry had to resign from the council a couple of years ago as he had angina, so it's just me waving the banner now. What are you doing down here anyway, you said you live in Patcham?'

'I had to visit an elderly lady in the flats at the bottom of Hove Street. She wanted to rewrite her will. I'm still at the solicitors. I have my own probate cases now, and I'm hoping to be a manager soon. So, while I was here, I thought I'd have a wander along the seafront. I'm so glad I did.'

'Me too. I remember you saying you were applying for a job with a firm of solicitors in Brighton and I said, how depressing, all those dead people.'

Jenny smiled at her friend. 'Yes, I remember you saying that too, and I'm still there. Let me write down my telephone number and address so we can keep in touch, I promise I will. But I'd better get back now. I wasn't expecting to stay down here so long.'

'Make sure you do this time. I want to hear more about this search, and, if you want to tell me, more about your birth mother. But before you go, tell me, is the sex still amazing with Martin? I certainly remember you telling me that.' She grinned at her friend.

Jenny nodded and returned her grin.

'Say no more, you lucky thing.'

9

Autumn 1991

A strengthening westerly wind threw Jenny's hair across her face as she locked her car. She had parked in the shadow of the sails of the windmill at West Blatchington. She walked across the small green to St Peter's church. Together with the mill, the church was all that remained of the downland hamlet, the manor house, farm and labourer's cottages having been demolished in the 1950s to make way for post-war housing, both council and private. The wooden windmill had been built in 1820. It had been a landmark for shipping in the channel and was painted by John Constable when he had lived in Brighton for a while, hoping to improve his wife's health. From this height, Jenny could see across the twin towns of Brighton and Hove to the Channel beyond. Opening the wooden gate to the churchyard, she walked across to her parents' grave. It had been ten years this month since they had died within two weeks of each other. It had been a difficult time, and she couldn't have coped without Rob's help. She knelt at the end of the stone edging to their grave and placed the bunch of chrysanthemums on the gravel.

Well, Mum, I finally made it to South Africa this year, ten years after you told me to go and find my father, but a lot has happened in the meantime and it's best that you were not around, as I know you would have disapproved. I know you loved Rob – more than I did, that's for sure – he was the son you would have had if your baby had lived. But I couldn't help myself, although I know you would have said that I could. Rob's a good man. You were right about that, and he probably didn't deserve me. Anyway, I'm pleased you enjoyed the best years of being grandparents to Lorna and Nicky. Life is not always easy for either of them now they are older, and they certainly don't make life easy for me. I blame myself sometimes – well, no – quite a lot of the time.

Jenny picked up the flower container at the head of the grave and, walking over to the tap by the gate, she spotted the red roof of what had been Martin's parents' bungalow. It lay in the middle of a crescent just south from the windmill. They had moved back to Hove from Southampton once Ricco had taken early retirement. When she was a teenager, they had lived in the centre of Hove, but Ricco had told her they had always preferred this area. She remembered the day she had met Martin again. It was here in the churchyard, and she was visiting her parents' grave. It was a dark afternoon and drizzling, and she hadn't noticed that there was anyone else around. He came over to warn her that she had left the lights of her Morris Minor on; she was always doing that. He was the last person she had expected to see, as, years earlier, when as teenagers they had been going out for a few weeks, he had moved to Southampton with his family, so she assumed he was still living there. 'You will wait for me, won't you?' he had asked her after they had been on a cycle ride together, saying he would come back to see her as often as he could. But she had only heard him say he was leaving, so with tears streaming down her face, she had rushed home, leaving him calling out her name as she disappeared from his view.

Sun was breaking through the clouds as she placed the vase containing the flowers at the head of the grave and pulled up a few shoots of groundsel that had grown in between the gravel. She stood up slowly, sighed and, following a pied wagtail up the concrete path to the gate, left the churchyard. Deciding to drive the long way home, she turned right at the nearby traffic lights and drove up the appropriately and locally named Snakey Hill, then turned left towards the Devils Dyke. She loved the view from here. On her right – on the northern ridge of the Downs – stood the twin windmills of Jack and Jill, while to her left lay downland, cultivated fields and the English Channel. She parked at Saddlescombe, a farming hamlet in the valley of the Dyke, virtually unchanged for centuries and now owned by the National Trust to conserve it for posterity. Walking on the flint-strewn path that formed part of the South Downs Way, she passed the duck pond and the ancient farmhouse, and walking towards the farm workers' cottages saw what she had come to see. On the telephone wires above her sat at least fifty chattering house martins gathering together as they prepared for their journey to South Africa for the winter. *I must be satisfied with what I have found out so far*, she thought. *Martin's right, I must give up searching – at least for a while.*

10

Spring 2006

The doorbell rang a second time, but Jenny continued to stare at the computer screen.

'Martin, door,' she shouted down the stairs. She knew it was Daniel. She had liked him when he was a boy and made him welcome on the weekends he stayed with them. But, now, although she tried hard not to, she resented the man he had become, with his broad grin and dark eyes, so reminiscent of Ricco, Martin's father, his success in life contrasting with her own children's lives and the worry they gave her. Lorna's had turned into a disaster zone – not that Lorna thought that. A single mother with two young children, she had dropped out of university to move in with Liam, who promptly walked out after their second baby arrived to set up home with her best friend. Jenny blamed herself, deciding that it was because of her leaving Rob that Lorna had craved a secure family life, which had turned into anything but. Nicky, who had spent his weekdays with Rob, and alternate weekends with herself and Martin, had at the age of eleven initially seemed unperturbed by his parents' separation and said he liked Louise. But once Rob had married her, he told Jenny how her attitude towards him changed, and he was made to feel that he was always in the way. After his half-brother was born, this feeling became worse. He had always been an academic child, but he didn't perform to his school's high expectations, and although allowed to go into the sixth form to retake a couple of his GCSEs along with two A levels, he seemed to drift and became friendly with a boy who was a regular cannabis user. So, lacking even less application to his studies than before, he was eventually asked to leave the school. He worked for just over a year as a trainee estate agent, then, one day, walked out of the office without leaving them or Jenny and Rob with any explanation to became a semi-permanent traveller in Asia, probably taking various chemical substances en route. Jenny didn't like to dwell on how he funded his travelling, so had never asked. Despite his assurances of how cheap it is to live out there, Jenny thought that cheap doesn't mean without some cost. Without forewarning, he would turn up on either her or Rob's doorstep to stay for a few days, before disappearing again. A Cambodian monastery was the last place he had mentioned, saying he was hoping to seek enlightenment by becoming a Buddhist and where she assumed he still was. Although his enlightenment didn't travel as far as her and Rob, resulting in them being permanently worried about him. Daniel, meanwhile, had completed his electrical engineering degree at Brighton University, had a well-paid job with British Telecom, a new-build house in Lewes, a loving wife and two children; a boy and a girl, of course.

Jenny had often wondered, if she had had siblings, whether an aunt or uncle's presence and input, especially when they were teenagers, would have helped them cope and lightened her load. The saying *it takes a village to raise a child* often came into her mind. Rob's younger sister Corinne had been a useless aunt. They had been lucky to get a birthday card from her. She preferred joining any protest group going. Rob said she had exited the womb protesting and had never stopped. Jenny often wondered, *why did I ever think that once children were eighteen, you waved them off into a permanent happy ever after? How could I have been so naïve?* Legal parental responsibility may cease, but never the worry and anxiety.

Once, she had thought that there was nothing that could come between herself and Martin, but she had been wrong about that too. She was depressed for hours after Daniel's visits. Martin had learnt to leave her alone until the black cloud had lifted. She would then seek him out, put her arms around him and say, 'Let's go for a walk on the Downs and have a drink somewhere,' and their life together would be good again, until Daniel's next visit. She marvelled how Martin never seemed to resent the many handouts they gave to Lorna. He was so good with her while she seemed only to just tolerate him. She wondered if she would be so generous if their roles were reversed and decided she wouldn't. She knew Martin had wanted another child. He had often told her of his wish for a child of their own. The first time he mentioned the subject was soon after they had moved into their current cottage, and the last time before they went to South Africa. She remembered each time he had broached the subject. She always spoke of her age being a drawback and the financial implications if she had to leave her job. She couldn't and didn't want to dismiss his wish for a child out of hand, so always said she would think about it. Then, when they discussed it later, Martin reluctantly agreed with her reasons not to go ahead. So, with efficient contraception, pregnancy was avoided. Then, when her periods became scantier and eventually disappeared, she could finally relax. Their sexual relationship was still necessary and fulfilling, but with her drop in libido – *thank God for oestrogen pessaries* – and the travelling involved with Martin's promotion to be a scientific officer for Natural England – the latest renaming of the original Nature Conservancy Council – those times were fewer than she would have liked. Often, it seemed easier to satisfy each other without full intercourse. Jenny didn't mind but knew Martin missed the bodily closeness. She often thought back to the early years of their relationship and smiled as she remembered when they couldn't keep their hands off each other.

'Bye, Jenn. We're just off, be back around six. I'll pick up some fish and chips for the three of us,' Martin shouted up the stairs.

Jenny carried on reading the words that flashed up on the computer screen. *Trace Your Family With DNA* and below were stories of how adopted people had found their birth family through the site – Find Your Ancestors. *I must try this*, she thought, thinking how, since their visit to South Africa years ago, she had from time to time tried every new avenue she could think of, from writing to South African Ex-Servicemen's Association, who sent her their quarterly magazines, to contacting a professor of genetics, who, having more important things to do with his time, never replied. *I'm sure I have brothers or sisters somewhere*, she thought, *my father was only young, a volunteer in the war, he would almost certainly have married and had a family. I must find them.*

11

Spring 2007

Jenny's heart leapt as she saw the name of a second cousin appear on the computer screen under her DNA relatives. *My closest relative yet, and she lives in Cape Town*, she thought, clicking on the icon above the name Bernadette Laubser. *What shall I say? Nothing too heavy. Why not? I'm not going to get anywhere by not saying the truth.* She took a deep breath and typed that she was searching for her birth father, and did Bernadette know of anyone in her family who had been a POW in the Second World War? Even if she didn't, could she provide the names of her grandparents and great-grandparents? Jenny read and reread her e-mail, replacing one word and then another until she was satisfied. She clicked 'send' and, leaning back in her chair, lifted a mug of tea to her lips, her face wrinkling as she felt the cold liquid.

For the past year, she had e-mailed all third and fourth cousins who appeared with worrying regularity in her list of closest relatives, hoping they had some links to South Africa that would give her hope. Two replied that they had, and the surname McKay had appeared in three fourth cousins' family trees. Life histories and family trees were e-mailed back, and the same John McKay, a coloured ancestor – living in the Karoo in the 1840s – was confirmed between them. But, with so many descendants and marriages, the trail went cold.

*

Jenny wandered along the path through the Wildlife Trust's Nature Reserve, feeling pleased with herself as she recalled sending Bernadette her e-mail that morning. A chiffchaff high in a tree that was not yet in full leaf, accompanied her, uttering his two-syllable song. Being a weekday, there was no one else around, but she always felt completely safe here. She reached a shiny, wooden seat by a large, boggy area thick with reeds that surrounded a pond and read the inscription on a brass plate on the back of the seat, dedicating it to the memory of an Edith Watson. She thought she might mention to Martin that she would like something similar when she died, as she received so much pleasure from visiting the reserve, especially in difficult times. Martin would almost certainly tell her not to be so morbid, but how could giving pleasure to people be morbid? Sitting down, she stared into the reeds and, hearing soft tweets, raised her binoculars and searched low down in the thick stems. She had read that there were sedge warblers in this pond. Ten minutes later, a glimpse of brown. *Yes, there he is, my first ever sighting.*

*

'Here you go.' Jenny handed Martin a glass of lager as he entered the kitchen.

'What's this for? I don't usually get this treatment on your day off. What have you done?' He grinned.

'I haven't done anything, but someone in Cape Town has. There's been a breakthrough at last.'

12

'I saw her, Jenny. I actually saw her; she's alive and well,' whispered Maureen as she leaned forward in her chair to be closer to Jenny.

'I don't understand; how could you find her?' Jenny asked, noticing that Maureen was wearing a scarlet jumper that shouted to the world that her mood had changed. At all previous meetings she had always worn dark clothes – mourning clothes, Jenny had thought. She recalled that at their last gathering, Maureen had whispered that she had heard from a woman at the birth mother's group she attended about a loophole in the system. Something to do with the reference on Maureen's daughter's NHS medical card, which had been allocated at her birth and could be matched up with her adoption certificate to enable her to know her daughter's adoptive surname and the address of her parents. Jenny had nodded to show her interest but quickly dismissed it from her mind. She had heard about possible loopholes before, but never one that she knew was possible.

'You know I mentioned that loophole I was told about?'

'Yes, I do remember, but I've never heard of it before or anyone using it to find their child's adoptive name.'

'Well, someone helped me. That's all I can say to you, and I did. I found out her new surname – they kept Sarah, the name I gave her, as her middle name, which was lovely – and her parents' address; they still live in the same house as they did when they adopted her, which is a miracle. So, early one morning, I drove to Dorking, that's where they live, and parked in the road just along from their house. Then, at just past eight o'clock, she came out and started walking to the station, obviously going to work. Amazingly, she still lives there with her parents, Jenny, so, I followed her.' She continued breathlessly, 'This means I can see her anytime I want to, isn't that fantastic? She looks just like I did at her age: quite tall, olive skin and dark hair, that's my Maltese heritage coming out.'

'I'm so pleased for you, Maureen, but you won't approach her yourself, will you? You mustn't. She might not know she's adopted.'

'No, of course not. I'm just so thrilled to have seen her. I might ask an intermediary to write to her later on. She is an adult, after all, and can make up her own mind about me.' Her eyes shined at Jenny for the first time as she continued, 'I've been so worried all these years that she may have died and I would never know.'

'I know, I do sympathise, and I do think that if that had happened, there should be some way for the birth mother to be informed. It would be very cruel for you and any other mother never to know. You look as if a great weight has been lifted off you.'

'It has, Jenny, it really has. I feel years younger as well.'

'Well, would you like something stronger than coffee this evening? I've a bottle of sherry on the sideboard. I'll offer some to Briony and anyone else who comes.'

'Yes, I'd love a glass, but how's your search going?' Maureen added as Jenny stood up and started walking over to the sideboard at the far end of the room.

'Really well. After all these years, I'm quite excited about it. I think I mentioned that I had joined Find your Ancestors, the DNA site. Well, a lady has contacted me from Cape Town, and I'm pretty sure it's the right family. She's been matched as my second cousin, so I'm finally getting somewhere at last.'

'I'm so pleased for you. You work so hard, trying to find birth relatives for everyone else. Where's Martin this evening? He's always out when we come round.'

'Yes, I'm afraid he is. Too many chatty women around, he says. Although that's not always the case. Tony comes sometimes. Martin's gone to Lewes for a drink with his son. He won't be late, so you should see him if you hang around. Anyway, enjoy your sherry,' Jenny said as she handed Maureen her glass. 'I'll make us some coffee later.'

There was a ring on the doorbell. 'I think that's Briony at the door. She said she would be late. I'd better go.'

'I'm so glad you could make it tonight,' Jenny said as she greeted Briony. 'Look, why don't you come into the kitchen with me first. I've just opened a bottle of sherry, so I'll pour you one unless you'd rather have some juice? Take your coat off and leave it on the dining chair.'

'I was in two minds about coming tonight, Jenny,' Briony said as she placed her coat over the chair and then ran her fingers through her hair. Jenny noticed she had lost weight and now looked a dead ringer for Kate Moss. 'No, sherry's fine.'

Jenny pulled out a chair for Briony at the kitchen table. 'I'm so sorry that I had to phone you with the bad news.' Three months earlier, she had suggested to Briony that, if she agreed, she could help her search for her half-sister, who had been born five years after Briony and was proving difficult to find. So, she had offered to do one last search herself. But she discovered that the child – Katrina Ann – had died shortly after her birth, resulting in her death being registered in the same quarter that her birth had been registered, and that was the reason why Briony had no luck in searching for her. Like most people, she had started searching for any death registration of her relative in the quarter following the birth registration, not thinking that she would have died so soon after birth. So Briony's years of searching for her half-sister had come to nothing.

'I'm sorry I broke down on the phone. I was pinning all my hopes on finding Katrina and speaking to her about our mother. Now I know why there was no trace of her anywhere.'

'I know, it was such a blow for you to hear that. But at least I found out from the ship's passenger lists that your mother did go to Australia with that German writer she was living with, and as far as we know, she's still there. So your search can still carry on, Briony. I know it's not easy with her being in Australia, but there is so much more information on the internet now, and more is being added all the time. In fact, a paid researcher I know is not getting nearly so much work now, because adoptees, if they can, are doing the research themselves once they know their birth family's name. Also, you never know, she might in the future place her name on the Government Contact Register for birth relatives that they introduced in 1991, so please don't give up hoping, and I'm around if you want to chat about it at any time. Do you remember I mentioned that I was thinking of leaving my job and becoming a paid researcher? But with the work drying up, I won't be doing that now. So, I'm stuck at the solicitors for evermore. Look, take your time with your sherry, I'll put some biscuits out and go back to the meeting and you can follow me when you feel ready.'

'Well, you've got your own research to do, Jenny, and like mine, yours isn't easy either. So perhaps it's as well that you're not going to be a paid researcher. By the way, is that Maureen sitting under the window? I didn't recognise her in that bright jumper.'

13

'It's a bit difficult, Lorna. I know it's my day off, but there is something I need to do today. Isn't there anyone else who can step in? I know it's difficult for you, but...' Jenny stopped herself from saying that *it would be a lot easier if you hadn't had children with that waste of space.* But the last time she had spoken in anger at her daughter's choice, Lorna had retaliated, accusing her of ruining her teenage years by leaving Rob, thereby forcing her into the arms of Liam.

'I suppose I could have them this afternoon. I can come over to yours at two. No, it's not too much trouble. Don't say that. Of course I love them, they're my grandchildren, and I'm not always making excuses, I did have something planned.' Jenny sighed. How could Lorna think that she didn't love Storm and Hector – *over-dramatising everything as usual.* She would have died for them, although she often wondered what had possessed Lorna and Liam to call their children those names, but Storm's name was surprisingly apt, and she hoped that Hector wasn't going to live up to his name either. But the reason for her reluctance to help, apart from the fact that she wanted to spend some time on her computer today, was that she found childcare boring and repetitive, and since Lorna had recommenced a degree course at Sussex University as a mature student, she was often being called on for childcare on her day off. It was Groundhog Day. It didn't seem that long ago that she was being pestered by Lorna or Nicky. 'Do it again, Mummy, do it again,' they would cry, and she had willingly obliged, crawling around the floor on all fours roaring like a lion. But second time around, she was in no hurry to repeat the exercise. But, that old slave master – guilt – was the more powerful.

*

'No, I'm sorry, Martin, look, I've just got back from helping Lorna. I must check this website. I noticed something this morning, it's important, but I had to leave it.'

'You're becoming obsessed again by this search. Surely it can wait another day? We agreed we'd eat out tonight.'

'And we would be if I hadn't had to look after Storm and Hector at short notice until seven. We can always go another evening.'

'You said that last week. You could have said no to Lorna, because we'd arranged to go out.'

Martin's words followed Jenny up the stairs. She sat at her desk in their bedroom, switched on the computer and clicked on Favourites, where she had saved the Thomas family tree that she had been sent that morning. She scanned the many branches, which covered the last two hundred years. The sash window rattled as the front door slammed. She stood up and, looking out of the window, saw Martin striding up the hill towards his Land Rover. A memory surfaced of a recent conversation when he had mentioned Izzy's name rather too many times. She had often wondered why the girl – sorry, woman – still worked with Martin at Natural England after all these years. Usually, graduates moved on after four or five years, but she had stayed. Martin said he worked well with her, and that she was well liked by everyone at the office, causing Jenny to become obsessed with the woman, especially as her blonde hair was exactly the same colour as Marilyn's. On one of her days off, she had spent hours waiting in her car outside his office but saw nothing to substantiate her jealousy; but just because she didn't see anything that day, didn't mean she could stop worrying. *I am obsessed with Izzy*, she thought. The very word that Martin used about her search, as, since Bernadette had sent the names of her relatives, she hadn't thought of much else and decided she must have an obsessive personality. Jenny relaxed back into her chair and continued paging up and back through the family tree, and then stopped. 'John McKay,' she said out loud. Glancing at his date of birth, she realised this was the same John McKay that her fourth cousins had mentioned, and they suggested in their e-mail yesterday that she look at this new family tree. *Another step closer*, she thought. *With Bernadette's great-grandparents and grandparent's names, perhaps now it's just a process of elimination by age and sex.*

One hour later, Jenny went back downstairs, poured a pile of cornflakes into a bowl and added some skimmed milk for her dinner. After tidying up, she went into the sitting room, turned the TV on and waited for Martin to return from wherever he had gone. At ten o'clock, she heard his Land Rover screech to a halt outside. She ran upstairs to the bathroom, found her oestrogen pessaries in the cabinet and, undressing down to her bra and panties, sat on the bed reading. She would call down to him when he came in and suggest they have an early night.

14

Jenny loved her work at the solicitors and enjoyed the company of her colleagues. 'Probate, that's all gloom and doom, isn't it? All those dead people.' She always smiled when she remembered Gail's words, because it wasn't the dead that Jenny had to deal with. It was the living that were the problem. She had been probate manager for the past ten years and saw the best and worst of humanity. Most relatives were genuinely sad at their loss, and if executors, did their best to ensure their late relative's wishes were carried out, while a few did their best to ensure that they weren't. They instructed their own solicitor to contest the will, ensuring that, like Dickens' *Jarndyce v Jarndyce*, there was very little left for any beneficiary to enjoy, leaving only sufficient for her own firm's fees. The cases she enjoyed most were when a large tranche of an estate was left to a charity. She imagined the delight on someone's face as they opened the envelope and saw the cheque and realised what a difference this legacy would make to someone's life.

Martin was not old enough to retire, and probably never would, even when he reached pension age. Conservation was his life. She knew that and always encouraged him.

He had often told her he would still carry on with his work after retirement age, but as a volunteer with the local wildlife trust. Jenny also had no wish to retire completely. Perhaps, if the partners agreed, she could drop down a day to three days a week sometime. Anyway, they still needed to meet their mortgage payments and offer more than occasional financial support to Lorna and Nicky. Because of these commitments, Jenny decided she would ask the partners if she could take six months' unpaid leave, so they could enjoy some long weekends away visiting a few European capitals.

*

Two months later, they arrived home early one morning after pounding the streets of Budapest for four days, and both feeling several kilos heavier due to devouring several calorie-filled lángos and bowls of goulash. As soon as their front door closed behind her, Jenny rushed upstairs to switch on the computer and scroll through any new family trees that had been added. One surname leaped out at her. Gordon Rous Barron – 1915 to 1992. Her heart stopped. She could hear shouting from downstairs, but Martin's words were as muffled as though he was still in Budapest.

Barron, that's one of Bernadette's family names. She's never mentioned a Gordon though, but I'm sure Rous is one of the names on the Thomas family tree with McKay. She stared at the sparse branches of a family tree that had just been placed on the site by a Madeline Pearson née Barron. Jenny clicked on the Thomas tree, confirming that several family members had the surname Rous. Was this the name that could link her to both her cousins? I have to prove it though. She walked over to the chest of drawers, her heart drumming against the walls of her chest, and pulled out a folder. Flicking through the National Archive documents, she found the lists of British and Commonwealth POWs that she had printed off years earlier; there were six Barrons listed, including a GR Barron. Searching through the folder again, she removed another list of the personal records of prisoners, seized from the liberated camps by the Russians and that the Soviet government under President Yeltsin had agreed to return to the UK. Again, there was a GR Barron listed with an address in South Africa and the name of his wife as next of kin. She also removed a page listing names of South African researchers. *I mustn't get my hopes up*, she thought, *Barron is quite a common name.*

The following day, Jenny stared at the grey headstone with black lettering in West Blatchington churchyard. Alice Porter, 1903 to 1981, and Frederick Porter, 1902 to 1981, both dead within two weeks of the other. She remembered her adoptive father with his many army reminiscences from spending over twenty years as a regular soldier. The army had been his life. His memories were mostly from India, Nowshera, on the north-west frontier area where he had been based for several years in the 1930s. As a child, she would squirm with embarrassment as he would tell his tales to anyone he encountered who would pretend to be interested. 'By God, those Pathan tribesman were good marksmen. We lost Nobby Baxter on the Khyber Pass. He only peeked out from this bloody boulder for a second, thinking there was no one around, and he was a gonna.' Then her mother Alice, whose years of illness outnumbered her well years. She remembered the cruel words she had said to her. 'I don't want to keep seeing you, I don't need you anymore.' She had shouted the words to her mother out of frustration when she had once again – unnecessarily – been jealous of the time she was spending with Rob's family. She wished she had never said them. How could she have been so cruel? She could have been nicer to her mother, but what child is? She had only realised the probable cause of all her mother's ailments when it was too late. Does any woman ever recover from the loss of her stillborn only child?

'I might be closer to finding him, Mum,' she whispered, remembering her mother's words as she lay dying.

'He was from South Africa. You must go and find your father.' Jenny stood up and looked across at the back of the windmill, perched high on a flint barn, its sails now fixed permanently and restored. It had been a friend and constant presence during her childhood. It was under these sails that Martin told her that he was moving away with his family. She walked to the edge of the graveyard and under the surrounding flint wall stood another headstone, black with gold lettering. She read: Ellen Mary Barretti, 1915 to 1978, and Enrico Barretti, 1917 to 1990. *So long ago now*, she thought. She remembered Martin telling Ricco soon after they had started living together that as soon as their divorces were finalised, they were going to be married, that was what they both wanted. Friends had often jokingly asked over the years, 'When are you two lovebirds going to tie the knot then?'

And Martin always replied, 'Two messy divorces are enough to put anyone off the idea. Anyway, why spoil a good thing, eh, Jenn?' and she would nod in agreement.

15

2007

Five words spoken twenty-six years ago had led to this.

'Thank you,' she whispered, 'thank you.' Barker the cocker spaniel in the cottage next door lived up to his name by seemingly echoing her gratitude.

'Shut up, shut up,' her neighbour shouted his usual rebuke.

Jenny stared at the screen for several minutes, then stood up. She felt her legs weaken so gripped the front of her computer desk. She took six deep breaths in and then slowly out to calm herself while looking out of her bedroom window at the parish church across the road. She thought of Toby the mongrel dog they had years ago and whose ashes were scattered in the churchyard they had often strolled through on their walks. But this morning, being midday, there was nobody about. *I need a drink*, Jenny thought, moistening her dry lips with her tongue. She walked out of her bedroom, to the top of the stairs, and, holding onto the banister – something that she hardly ever did – stepped carefully down each wooden step. She walked through the sitting room that stretched the length of the cottage and into a side extension that contained the kitchen. Opening the fridge, she reached for a bottle of sparkling water. 'No, you idiot, not today,' she mumbled and pulled out a bottle of Chardonnay – which they were saving for a friend's party – instead. Picking up a wine glass from the worktop, she filled it to the top, walked across to the back door, sat down on the wooden bench in the tiny lobby and stared into the garden at the holly tree which gave their cottage its name and in winter was covered with berries. It stood against a crumbling brick wall that surrounded the narrow garden. She sipped her wine and wondered who she would tell first, then decided she didn't want to tell anyone. Not Lorna, who wouldn't be interested; not Nicky, who would; and not even Martin, who had supported her throughout her search. At least not yet. It was her discovery and hers alone. She thought that this must be how Victorian plant hunters must have felt at the end of their lifetime quest for some exotic rare species, as they knelt in front of their precious find in some remote corner of the globe, wanting to keep their discovery to themselves, for as long as possible. To share it would spoil the moment and the time when only they knew. A pleasure similar to sexual fulfilment.

*

This was the place she wanted to be this afternoon. She locked her car and wandered southwards along the lane that edged the common. Cow parsley was now at full height and lined the lane with their lace blooms. She passed a detached Tudor-beamed house and read the name on the gate –

Quince Cottage. *Not exactly a cottage now*, Jenny thought; probably enlarged from two or three smaller cottages. A jay screeched and, with a flash of blue, flew across her path from a hawthorn tree. She walked on for a quarter of a mile until she reached an overgrown footpath that led to Edburton – a scattering of cottages that lay under the Devil's Dyke – and where a spring gushed from deep in the chalk and was now a trickle that edged the footpath. Time to turn back. A flute-like whistle came from deep in the scrub to her left. She stopped and recognised the unmistakable sound of a nightingale. *I love this place. He must be as happy as I am today as he waits for a mate to join him.* She stood in the sunshine and listened as the bird completed his repertoire, before walking to her car and driving home.

She went upstairs, restarted the computer and scrolled down reading the many pages of Gordon Rous Barron's estate documents. The death notice and accompanying documents that the researcher had sent her confirmed that Gordon's mother's maiden name was Elizabeth Georgina Rous, the same lady as on the Thomas family tree. His father was a Hugh Barron. Bernadette's great-uncle. The link had finally been confirmed. She noticed that he had been married twice, his first wife having died young, leaving two small boys. On a separate page were stated beneficiaries. Five names were listed with their dates of birth: Andrew Barron, born in 1940, just before Gordon had volunteered to fight, and Alastair Barron, born in 1947. Then a gap of five years before Madeline and Catherine Barron – twins – were born, and seven years later, his youngest child, Vanessa Barron. *Just as I have always wished, I have got sisters, three of them.*

16

'What! You've known for nearly a week, Jenny, and after all your years of searching, you didn't tell me. I can't believe it,' Martin shouted at Jenny over his plate of spaghetti as she blurted out that she had finally found her birth father and his family.

'I know it must be hard for you to understand, but I think it's because it has taken me so long to find them, I just needed to live with it myself for a while. To get used to the idea, I suppose. I can hardly believe it myself still.'

'I wondered why there's a bottle of Cava on the table.'

'There's often a bottle of something on the table, Martin. We don't need a reason. I'll get the flutes and we can celebrate together.'

'No, I'll do that. Just let me take a couple of mouthfuls of this first, I'm starving. Your spaghetti looks almost as good as Papa's.'

'Only almost? Well, he was a good cook, wasn't he?' Jenny thought back to their many lunchtime visits to Enrico in the years before he died, and how he always gave her a quizzical look when she walked into his house, as though trying to decipher what it was about her that disturbed him. Martin said he always had an eye for the ladies and there were often explosive rows at home when he was growing up.

'There's something else as well. I have two brothers and three sisters, and two are twins.'

'For God's sake, Jenny, you kept that to yourself too. I'm starting to wonder what else you haven't told me if you can keep all this to yourself for days. I didn't suspect anything. You just seemed your usual infuriating self. Which two are twins, the girls or the boys?'

Feeling herself redden, Jenny got up from the table and, lowering the oven door, stared into the empty oven. She took three deep breaths and returned to her chair. 'The older two girls.'

'I knew you were contacting that woman in Cape Town, but that was a while ago. You haven't said much about it lately.'

'Yes, the researcher. I was getting so close, I didn't want to tempt fate, in case I was wrong.'

'Look, almost finished.' Martin smiled and looked up at Jenny. 'Sorry, I was so hungry; that's being out all day over at Seaford Head. All that sea air. I'll pour the Cava now. You finish your spaghetti, then you can tell me all about it.'

Jenny only managed to eat a few mouthfuls, saying that the neighbourhood fox could have the rest. Then, cradling their glasses of Cava, they walked through into the sitting room.

'My God, Jenn, let me give you an enormous hug.'

They clung together in the centre of the room before sitting down on the sofa, with Jenny sharing the estate documents sent by the researcher with Martin. 'Hang on, let me get my glasses. So, he's dead, your father? That's a shame you'll never get to meet him.'

'Yes, but that wasn't a surprise after all these years, and if he hadn't died, I would never have been sure that I had the right man, because the South African Estate documents prove his connection to Bernadette through his father and the McKays through his mother.'

'I still can't believe this, Jenn. You always wanted brothers and sisters, didn't you?'

'Well,' Jenny hesitated, 'sisters anyway, because I was an only child. But brothers should be fun. I never in a million years thought there would be five siblings. Two, or maybe three, but Gordon was married twice; his first wife died young, leaving Andrew – he was born in 1940 – and Alastair, who was just a toddler. That must have been so hard for all of them. Then he married Marion and had the twins, Madeline and Catherine, and seven years later, Vanessa. The documents state their full names, including married names and dates of birth, but no addresses.'

'That must have been such a shock seeing the names of his children.'

'Yes, I still can't believe it. How do I become a sister? What do I do? I don't know.'

'Well, I shouldn't worry too much about that, they're not here, are they? I suppose we had better start saving; I can see another trip to South Africa on the horizon. It's a good job you've taken a few months off work.'

'Yes, I'll have to use the same researcher to help me find them.'

'You could always check out Facebook first. It's worth a try and might save you, or rather us, quite a bit of money. But I still can't get over why you didn't tell me before, Jenn. Anyway, congratulations, you certainly deserve it after all these years; talk about persistent, you'll win prizes for that.' Martin lifted his glass to meet Jenny's. 'There's something else. I owe you an apology. I always said you would never find him without a name, didn't I? Well, I was wrong. I admit it.'

'No, you were right when you said it. I couldn't have found him back then. It's only because of advances in DNA and the ancestry site, and also because he's dead. Even if I thought it was him by elimination of close relatives, I would never have known for sure if he hadn't died.'

Martin jumped up from the sofa. 'I'm going to fetch the bottle, let's empty it. There will never be better reason.'

Part Two

17

2007

'Rockall – wind north west backing south west later four to six, sea moderate to rough, showers, rain later, visibility good, occasionally poor. Malin – wind north west backing south west later three to five, sea moderate occasionally slight in east later...' The dulcet tones of the broadcaster had failed to lull Jenny into sleep. She switched the radio off and squinted in the darkness trying to see the time on the clock. She could just make out one-twenty and turned over in bed for what seemed like the twentieth time, then, sitting up, she reached for the book she had been reading for her next book club meeting and switched on her bedside light. Martin snored gently beside her. *How can he sleep?* she thought, resenting his peace of mind. Half an hour later, she dropped the book onto the floor and, falling back on to her pillow, slept until six o'clock when she woke with a start as the alarm pieced her ears. Sitting on the edge of the bed for a few minutes, she imagined the day ahead, then, slipping into her dressing gown, she walked out of the bedroom and downstairs to make herself a cup of tea.

*

Jenny peered into the mirror of the supermarket toilet and made last-minute touches to her make-up. She thought she was being more particular about her looks than if she was meeting a prospective lover for the first time, her bowels turning and twisting as if in a dance, forcing her to put her make-up bag down and dash back into the cubicle for the third time. Then staring at her image in the long mirror, she drew a deep breath in and then out to calm herself and walked out to face the two women she had spotted earlier sitting on a sofa in the café alcove.

'Hello, I'm Jenny, you must be Madeline and Catherine.' Jenny smiled at her sisters as she sat down on an armchair and faced them across the low table. They were identical except for their hair and clothes. 'Thank you for meeting me. I can't believe you both live in England. It's unbelievable.'

'How could we not meet you after your e-mail? It's also unbelievable that you managed to find us after all those years of searching. I hope we're worth the effort. I'm Madeline,' said the twin with cropped, dark-brown hair flecked with grey. She was smartly dressed in a grey A-line skirt and pale-blue blouse that opened at the neck to reveal a string of pearls. 'Catherine phoned me as soon as she read your e-mail. I thought she had too much to drink when she told me.'

'Well, I had, Maddy, I needed a stiff drink after I read Jenny's e-mail. No, tell a lie, two drinks. I couldn't think what on earth it was all about at first. I had to read it three times before the penny dropped. We had no idea you existed.' Cathy ran her hands through her dark, wavy hair. She was also smartly dressed but in pale-blue jeans and a chunky, amber, hip-length jumper complimented by a matching amber necklace and large, gold, hooped earrings.

'Blame Facebook. It was Martin's idea – he's my partner. I just typed in Catherine's surname because it's so unusual. I couldn't believe it when your website came up with an address in England and not South Africa, and with your telephone number and e-mail address. I just love your paintings, by the way. You're such a good artist. But I don't understand, how come you both live here?'

'Well, Maddy has lived here the longest, about fifteen years now, isn't it? She married Chris, he's really a Christian not a Christopher, but he hates his name, doesn't he, Maddy? He's not at all religious – in fact, he's an atheist – but his parents were, religious I mean. The last time he set foot in a church was when you were married. You were over here working in London when you met him, weren't you? He's British, but after their marriage, they went back to live in South Africa. Me – call me Cathy – I married a Dutchman, hence the unpronounceable surname. Gerrit was working for Shell International in South Africa and other places, but as soon as his base moved to Holland about five years ago, we decided to join Maddy and Chris. Gerrit travels all over, so it doesn't really matter where we live, especially now the children are over eighteen.'

Maddy took up the conversation. 'The main reason we came here was that because our two children were born in South Africa, our son would have been drafted into the South African army when he was eighteen to fight in Angola. We couldn't let that happen, so with Chris being

British, it was easy for us to move here once he found a decent job.'

Jenny felt her nervousness melting away with Maddy's welcoming smile. 'Thank goodness you have completely different hairstyles; I wouldn't be able to tell you apart otherwise. Your features are absolutely identical.' She looked down at the custard tart they had bought for her but it remained on the plate. The bustle of the café in the early afternoon carried on unnoticed around the three of them as they revelled in hearing each other's stories.

'We may look identical but our personalities are very different. I'm the oldest by six minutes,' said Maddy.

'No, you're not, only by four minutes,' said Cathy. 'Those extra two minutes are important.'

'Tell me about the others.'

Cathy took up the conversation. 'Well, Andy – short for Andrew – lives in New Zealand, North Island, with his wife Gwen, and they have two children. He's the brainy one. Although he may have some competition now. He won't like that.' She giggled. 'He trained as a lawyer but ended up editing a local paper out there. He's retired now, but unfortunately, he was diagnosed with Parkinson's disease a few years ago, so you may not get to see him. They used to visit here every year, they came over last year, so you just missed him. But as far as we know, they're not coming this year. The boys' names are a nod to their Scottish roots. Their mother Peggy was born in Scotland and emigrated when she was small with her family in the 1920s.'

Maddy continued, 'Alastair – Al – he's the sporty one, easy-going and the image of Dad. He's lovely; we think he was Dad's favourite, mainly because he was so good at sport, especially cricket. He played for South Africa when the rebel teams toured over there. He lives in France now with Fleur and their four children.'

'France, why France?'

'Well, his wife Fleur works for an American company and their European headquarters were in Grenoble. They lived in the USA for six years but are back in France now. So nearer to us, which is good. They wanted to leave South Africa because of the apartheid regime. So you could say that Maddy and Alastair are apartheid refugees.'

'I can't believe you've all left South Africa.'

'At different times, of course, not all at once. It was very difficult living there in the '70s and '80s, none of us agreed with the regime. Dad was actually a member of the ANC at one stage, then changed to the Progressive Party. He was quite political. There was so much censorship when we were growing up – certain books were banned and films – we missed out on so much.'

'Not as much as the black and coloured people missed out on,' interrupted Cathy. 'Dad always encouraged us to travel. It was he who found Maddy a job in London with the Prudential, he was a manager for their Natal branch in South Africa, and I lived in Cyprus for a while nannying before I was married. Don't you want to hear about Gordon?'

'Yes, of course, but Vanessa, is she in England too?'

The twins exchanged glances. 'She lives in Nottingham. Well, she did when we last heard. She was the last of us to leave South Africa, that was soon after I left. Have you traced your birth mother?' Cathy asked.

'Yes, but she had died by the time I traced her. That was years ago.'

'Shame, so you didn't get to meet her? This is so exciting, isn't it, Maddy? What a pity that Dad's dead. I love it that he had an affair, so romantic. We could contact our local paper, Maddy, it's such a good story.'

'No, please don't do that. Anyway, I couldn't have contacted Gordon if he was still alive. I wouldn't have dared. It would have been too embarrassing for both of us. He may not have wanted to know me, or even worse, couldn't remember that he had ever met my birth mother, and what would I have done then? Anyway, I could never have found you if he hadn't died. I have copies of Gordon's Death Estate papers that the researcher found for me. You can see your names listed on the third page. There's a copy for each of you to keep.'

'We've never seen these, have we, Maddy? Although Al must have, I see he's signed the death certificate. We would have loved it if you had contacted Dad, wouldn't we? It would have been hilarious. He was such a stickler for behaving properly. Or what he thought was correct, and he was always certain he was right as well, very Victorian in his attitude.'

Jenny thought that Cathy seemed the more dominant and extrovert of the two, but Jenny could tell from their faces that both were finding it difficult to absorb all the information they were being told.

Maddy took up the conversation. 'Well, he wasn't perfect, although he always made out that he was. He had to get married to our mother. I never believed that we were premature, which was what we were always told. Not twins at six pounds something, which I was, and Cathy was five pounds something. I actually put a small family tree on an ancestry site. We never knew much at all about our relatives. We hardly ever saw them apart from his brother Brian, and we certainly never talked about family. I think Gordon fell out with most of them.'

'Yes, Maddy, it was your small family tree on the same ancestry site that I was a member of that led me to Gordon, his middle name of Rous was the connection. Now tell me more about Gordon?' Jenny, on hearing her stomach rumble, finally picked up her custard tart and relaxed into the supermarket armchair. 'I'm sorry about my stomach but thank you for the tart. I just couldn't eat anything this morning, I was so excited. I couldn't sleep either.'

'Neither could we,' they said together. 'But we'll all sleep well tonight.'

As she drove away from Horsham, Jenny basked in the information she now knew about her father. A love of literature, writing and learning. Also, her job at the solicitors was similar to her older brother's. Gordon was, however, quick-tempered and could be unkind, and often was to the twins' mother. Jenny recognised those traits in herself. Not in her relationship with Martin, but she had been unkind to Rob. She also remembered how quickly she would lose her temper with Lorna and Nicky when they were small and recalcitrant. It wasn't something she was proud of and she tried her best to forget those times. She was surprised that her love of nature had not been one of Gordon's traits, although the twins told her that Brian, his younger brother, had been a journalist with the *Cape*

Times and had written a weekly Nature Notes column for the paper. He had also published a book on the wildlife of the Kalahari. Jenny felt she had come home.

18

The following months passed in a whirl. Several e-mails were exchanged between the three sisters and invitations given to Jenny and Martin, and reciprocated, to visit to each other's houses for lunch and to meet their husbands and children. Then the most important thing of all for Jenny. Cathy had found a black-and-white photo of Gordon, smiling broadly and resplendent in his army uniform. Jenny poured over the photo at every opportunity, revelling in their facial similarities. The same slanting, grey eyes and even a mole on both of their faces. Every time she looked in the bathroom mirror, she saw him staring back at her. She was at ease in her sisters' company, even though they had grown up on different continents, and family characteristics, likes and dislikes from uncles and brothers, were noted and smiled over.

'You said Vanessa lives in Nottingham, Cathy. Do you have her address? I would like to contact her,' Jenny asked at one of their regular meetings at the supermarket café.

'I'll e-mail it to you,' said Maddy. 'Dale, her husband, sent it to Chris after they moved up there – they lived near us in Surrey when they first came over – but she's never written to us since they moved. Chris tries to contact them, usually around Xmas, but he's never had any response. You tried too, didn't you, Cathy? Though God knows why. So don't be too disappointed if you don't hear back, Jenny. They may have moved.'

'I must at least try. She's my sister too. Perhaps the shock of knowing I exist will make a difference.'

'Perhaps.'

A week after posting the letter to the address Maddy had given her, it was returned marked 'Return to sender, unknown at this address'.

'Well, she obviously doesn't want any contact with her family, does she?' said Martin, as Jenny showed him the envelope. 'Otherwise she would have given your sisters her new address. Just leave it, Jenny, you've found Maddy and Cathy, that was miracle enough, especially with them living here in England, and in the south east too. I couldn't believe it when you showed me Cathy's webpage. She may even have returned to South Africa.'

'I might just have one more try.'

'For God's sake, Jenny.' Martin raised his voice. 'You've spent years searching, why carry on? Be satisfied with finding your twin sisters and knowing you've got brothers. Aren't they enough for you? You're one of those annoying people who are always searching for something else, never satisfied with what you have. You're not really interested in them as people. You just like the thrill of the chase, then you lose interest. That's why you like birdwatching, always trying to find some elusive bird, like those twitchers.'

'That's a ridiculous comparison. Of course I'm interested in them, they're my sisters.' But Jenny recognised there was some truth in Martin's words. 'I haven't lost interest in you.'

'You didn't have to search for me though, did you?'

'No, I didn't.' Jenny remembered their chance meeting in the churchyard, which changed both their lives. 'I still love you, Martin, but I do know I can be annoying. Once I decide on something, I just can't let it go,' she whispered.

'So long as you can't let me go and you still fancy me. I can put up with annoying, come here.' Opening his arms wide, he moved forward to embrace her.

19

Late 2007

'Wow, come in. What a surprise, another sister. I couldn't believe it when I got your letter.'

Jenny smiled at the tall woman in front of her as she stepped over the threshold of the newly built semi. She noticed immediately the resemblance around her eyes to the twins. Vanessa was wearing a grey tracksuit top with matching bottoms and white trainers. Jenny felt distinctly overdressed in her best jeans, jumper and jewellery. Unsure whether to hug her or shake hands, she did neither.

'Well done for tracking me down. I should have let Cathy or Maddy know my address, they are family after all, but we've never been close, what with the age gap and them being twins.'

'Well, if it hadn't been for your elderly ex-neighbour letting me have your new address, I wouldn't be here. Luckily, he's lived in that house for years and was in the old street directory and phone book. I phoned him, but naturally he was reluctant to give me your address. Then when I sent him a copy of my letter to you, explaining we were half-sisters, he changed his mind.'

'Yes, he phoned me, so of course I said it was OK. I was close to his wife, still am. She was sorry I was moving away and has kept in touch. But I needed a fresh start after my divorce. Enough about me though, come on through, lunch is ready. I want to hear all about you. You're certainly good at research and finding people. You should work for the secret service, MI6 or MI5, whatever it's called.'

Jenny followed Vanessa into a spacious open-plan lounge/kitchen diner with white, bare walls that stretched the length of the house and minimal furniture. 'This is so spacious, so different to our house. We have a Victorian cottage, very cosy, but the rooms are small.'

'Well, when I decided to move, I wanted to go for something completely different from what my ex and I had. We had an older-style terraced house. This is modern and only has two bedrooms, that's all I need or can afford. So, you're married then, Jenny?'

'No, not anymore. I was years ago, but we divorced. We have two grown-up children though. I live with my partner Martin, we've been together for years but never got around to making it legal, so as good as.'

'You look like Dad. You have the same shape face and grey eyes. Mine are brown like my mother.'

'Maddy and Cathy said the same, and when they showed me his photo, it was like looking in the mirror.'

'Look, sit down and help yourself to crisps. I've a quiche and salad and some white wine in the fridge, I'll go and get them. We must celebrate. Thank God you're not a twin. When we were children and growing up in Pietermaritzburg, I always felt excluded by the twins. They were several years older than me but it was as if they were always enough for each other and didn't want or need anyone else. The boys had each other too, so they didn't want to play with me much either. Childish, I know, but true.'

'Yes, I can see how that could be,' Jenny said, thinking how different Vanessa seemed from her twin sisters apart from some physical resemblance. Over the following two hours, Jenny told her how for years she had tried to find her family and had finally been successful. 'It's amazing that you live in England too. It's just so unbelievable. You couldn't make it up, could you? They say truth is stranger than fiction. I'm so lucky. I thought I would have to travel to South Africa to find you all, and then I might never have been able to find you.'

'Well, it can be difficult to find anyone in South Africa. The records are not as good as here. I was always a sporty girl, athletics mainly. One-hundred metre sprint to be exact, that was my best distance, though I also ran the two hundred metres. Alastair is also sporty. He was excellent at cricket and rugby. Once apartheid ended, it was easier for me to travel abroad, so, after the rest of them left for one reason or another, there was nothing and nobody – apart from our mother – to keep me there. Dad had been dead for years by then. There were far more opportunities in coaching, etc. abroad, and I could get an Ancestry visa, as our grandfather on Dad's side was born in Durham. Relatives on our grandmother's side, though, have been in South Africa since the seventeenth century, the original Afrikaners.'

'Well, I was quite sporty too,' said Jenny. 'I represented my school in the one hundred metres; I came third, from what I remember. I was also the shooter for the school netball team and I was entered for the interschools swimming gala. My mother always said it was a shame that I gave up sport when I left school, but there were too many other distractions – like boys.' She grinned and thought that Vanessa definitely looked athletic. She was taller and slimmer than the twins and, much to Jenny's consternation, slimmer than herself. 'Look, Vanessa, I know we could talk for ages, and it's such a shame that we haven't had long together today, but I must keep an eye on the time. I need to catch the bus back to the station to make the five o'clock train to St Pancras. It's been quite a journey.'

'Yes, I'm sorry I couldn't collect you from the station, or give you a lift back, but I can't afford to run a car now I'm on my own.'

'Oh, don't worry about that, I've never been to Nottingham before, so I enjoyed catching the bus. It wasn't far. Everything here, especially the buildings, look so different from Brighton. The lunch was lovely, by the way.'

'That's the least I could do for you. I can't believe today has happened. Thank you so much for making the effort and coming up. Let me write my phone number down and you must do the same for me. Even if we can't meet up often, we can always chat.'

Jenny stared out of the train window at the flat East Midland countryside, mainly ploughed fields with an occasional red-brick farmhouse. So different from the rolling Downs she loved. She reflected on the afternoon and looked forward to discovering more about Vanessa in the months to come. She'd already decided not to tell Martin about her visit, justifying her decision by the fact that he didn't want her to find Vanessa in the first place, saying that two half-sisters in England must be enough for anyone.

20

'Yes, of course I'll come over.' Jenny sighed as she put the phone down. She knew the procedure. Nicky had been found shouting obscenities at a homeless man on the seafront at Worthing. The police had taken him into the station overnight for safe-keeping and phoned Jenny that morning. She went into the kitchen, removed a box of Olanzapine tablets from the drawer, grabbed her car keys and drove to Worthing to collect her son. She stopped at a local supermarket for a couple of ready meals and other necessities and then settled Nicky back into his supported accommodation. After cooking them both scrambled eggs for lunch and ensuring he had taken his medication, she left. She knew she would now have to call him each day to ensure he continued to take his antipsychotics. On his last trip home from Cambodia, he had stayed with her and Martin, sleeping on a sofa bed in the study on their second floor and telling them he had decided that he was staying in England for good. But four weeks later, he had a psychotic breakdown, almost certainly – at least, that was Jenny's theory – as a result of previous drug taking. Her hopes that he would finally settle down and find regular work now he was back vanished overnight. Unknown to Jenny, he left the house one evening carrying a kitchen knife. He threatened a local barman, as voices in his head were telling him that the barman, with his long, dark locks and beard, was a reincarnation of Rasputin. The police were called and he was sectioned, remaining an in-patient at Mill View Hospital for four weeks, when he was then assessed to be well enough to be discharged back into the care of Jenny and Martin until appropriate accommodation could be found for him.

Every day for the week following Nicky's overnight stay at the police station, Jenny walked on the Downs. Some days, she parked at the Jack and Jill Windmills above the village of Clayton and walked towards Ditchling Beacon for about a mile before turning back. Other days, she would walk from Ditchling Beacon, past the dew pond, in the direction of Lewes, until she saw trees planted in the shape of a V below the ridge above Plumpton, when she would then turn around and walk back to the car park. Walking and looking out over the Weald calmed her and was a distraction from worrying about Nicky. Martin was always sympathetic and helpful, but it didn't affect him in the same way it did Jenny. *I can't expect it to*, she thought, but it made her even more resentful of Daniel's seemingly perfect life. *At least Lorna is thriving*, she thought, *thank goodness she's nearly completed her degree.*

*

'I'm sorry I haven't phoned before, family troubles,' Jenny said to Vanessa at the end of the week. 'I meant to call you last week to see if we could arrange to meet up. It's been quite a while. How are you settling into your house?'

'It's OK, but I miss my old neighbours. Everyone here is younger and busy, they're either both out working all day or they have children. I only say hello to a few in passing. I was thinking I could meet you somewhere in London. I can't expect you to come all the way up here again. I need to know more about you.'

'Yes, and vice versa. I spent virtually all of our first meeting telling you how I found the family. What about next Tuesday lunchtime, if you can get the day off? We could meet at Victoria Station. I know a good café near there.'

Vanessa was waiting for Jenny outside the entrance to Smith's on the station concourse. Jenny walked across and greeted her with a hug. 'I didn't recognise you at first with your hair in a ponytail. It makes you look younger; sorry, that doesn't mean you looked older the other week. The coffee shop that I know is not far away. Shall we go?' Walking arm in arm, Jenny guided her sister to an Italian café in Wilton Street. 'I used to come here for lunch when I was doing my research. Let's sit by the window. We're lucky to get a seat at this time. I usually came a bit earlier.'

'You look well, Jenny. How's Martin? It is Martin, isn't it?'

'He's good, thank you. I'm ordering a coffee first, what about you?'

'Cappuccino would be good and a toasted mozzarella-and-tomato sandwich.' As Vanessa removed her coat, Jenny noticed she was wearing a light-blue tracksuit top with matching bottoms, which seemed incongruous in central London. She wondered if she ever wore anything else.

'I'll have the same then. So, it's taking you a while to settle in.'

'As I said on the phone, it's a challenge. It's been eight months now. Someone told me it takes two years before you can feel at home. Apart from missing my old neighbours – I could always pop in when things got difficult with Dale – it's hard living on my own, I never have before. I've just got to give it more time, that's all.'

'You have Jackie, your daughter, though.'

'Yes, but she's busy working. I told you, didn't I, that she lives in Birmingham? So I don't see a lot of her.'

'Yes, you did, it must be difficult. I wouldn't find it easy living on my own either. But I'm sure it will get better as time goes on. Good, that's quick. Here come our coffees and food. I left home in a hurry this morning, so I'm starving.'

Vanessa looked down at her cappuccino as she stirred two brown sugar lumps around. 'Have you seen the twins since we met?'

'No, not yet. We usually meet every three months or so, so I'll see them soon, definitely before Christmas.'

'They don't know that we've met then?'

'No, but I will tell them. I wouldn't feel comfortable if I didn't.'

'Well, I feel I must fess up, Jenny. The main reason I've never written to them, in case you think I should have and think badly of me, is because Cathy had an affair with Dale. It was a few years ago now, when we first came here.

She thinks I didn't know about it, but I did. It was before we moved to Nottingham. I think it had been going on for a few months. We lived in a rented flat quite close to both of them. I told you I managed to get an Ancestry visa. Well, Dale couldn't find work, so he was at home a lot, unhappy and bored. I found a part-time job in a local shop. I blame her for my marriage break-up. Once I realised what was going on, I found it hard to trust him after that. Dale ended the affair because I was offered my coaching job at Notts Athletic Club. So, it would have been difficult for them to carry on. I was always suspicious after that, looking for clues that he was seeing other women, you know, the usual things, looking in his pockets, checking his phone, and that's not attractive in a person, so we were always rowing. He found a job in security at a night club, of all places, so that didn't help, and I just couldn't stop checking up on him.'

'I can sympathise with that. I've been there myself.'

'But you and Martin are happy together?'

Jenny nodded. 'Yes, we are, but that doesn't stop you being jealous of other women. In fact, it makes it worse. Especially as we both left our marriages to be together. There is always the thought that as he left someone before, it could happen again with someone else.' She thought of Izzy, Martin's assistant, and how jealous she had been, and still was, when she thought of them working closely together.

'That must work both ways though.'

Jenny nodded. 'True.' Although she thought her colleagues in the probate department were unlikely candidates for an affair with her, or anyone else.

'I do blame Cathy for the break-up though. I understand how it happened. Dale was unhappy here. Never wanted to leave South Africa in the first place. He left a job he liked and was good at to come here. It was me who wanted to leave, and it took him a while to find any work that he wanted to do. The only people he knew at that time were the twins and their husbands. What I can't understand, though, is how quickly he found someone else once we decided to divorce. He lives in Derby now with this woman, probably met her at the night club. Men do, don't they? Find someone else quickly, I mean. Perhaps they're not so fussy as we are?'

'You're still young, Vanessa, and attractive. I'm sure you'll find someone else too. Give it time.'

'You mean, two years, like the house.' She grinned.

During the following hours in which they ordered two tiramisus and two further coffees, Jenny told Vanessa about her job and that at the moment she was enjoying six months' unpaid leave and after Xmas would only be working three days a week. She explained Martin's vocation with English Nature, how they had been childhood sweethearts and how they both loved the countryside. Vanessa reciprocated, describing her coaching sessions at Notts Athletic Club and her part-time admin job at Nottingham ice rink that she had taken to make up her salary. Then she added, 'That's strange, that you love the countryside, because I like nature too, but I don't find it that interesting around Nottingham. Don't get me wrong, I love the city itself and there's Sherwood Forest, of course, but I can't get excited about all those old oak trees, fantastic as they are, because I'm just not used to woods and forests. I find them claustrophobic. I'm used to the open veld and the Karoo, so different to England. Rutland Water is interesting, but too far away, especially without my own transport. Nottinghamshire isn't as varied as Surrey, where there was heathland and the North Downs. Obviously, I shouldn't compare England to South Africa at least here I don't have to worry about snakes. Perhaps it's genetic?'

'What's genetic? Love of the countryside? Oh, I don't know about that, Vanessa.'

'Well, our Uncle Brian, Dad's brother, was a journalist with the *Cape Times*. He wrote a book about the wildlife of the Kalahari.'

'Yes, the twins mentioned that. It sounds really interesting.'

'Well, I have a copy. I bought it with me when we came over. I'll lend it to you.'

Jenny smiled to herself as the Brighton train crossed the Balcombe Viaduct. She looked out at the fields of winter wheat, thinking this was her favourite view, and recalled her lunch with Vanessa. She was so pleased to meet up again with her, especially now she knew that they had an interest in common. The twins had never mentioned being interested in the countryside. Cathy was a brilliant artist, and Maddy was apparently an excellent bridge player, but their other interests, apart from golf, tended to be more domestic and social, not that it mattered, but sharing an interest made her feel closer to Vanessa. She could easily imagine how Dale had been tempted by Cathy, her vivaciousness and physical similarity to

Vanessa. How easily an affair could happen. He had been in a strange country where he hadn't wanted to be and finding it difficult to adjust, so naturally he would seek out fellow expats for support. But never a sister-in-law. Surely they were always off-limits, however attractive you might find them?

21

Spring 2008

'The dovecote is scheduled as an ancient monument. I don't expect you've ever seen one before. It was built in the seventeenth century in the grounds of this farmhouse.' The three sisters stood on the grassy bank peering over the flint wall at the dovecote. 'You see the row of new, terraced houses opposite? They were integrated into what was the longest tithe barn in Sussex,' Jenny explained as they stood at the top of Church Hill.

Turning to face the church, Cathy laughed and said, 'Do you think you'll end up in that churchyard?'

'Not decided yet, but probably not, I'm not religious.' Jenny grinned. 'But our old dog's ashes are scattered there. The church was originally built from local flints but, unfortunately, was later covered in that concrete, to protect it from the weather I suppose. There are plans to restore it to its original state. It has some ancient wall paintings that are being restored at the moment, and there used to be a duck pond in the grassy depression. That was before our time, though, the duck pond as well as the paintings.' She smiled. 'These cottages, including ours, are

Victorian, but a couple down the hill are older, Tudor, probably. One is supposed to be the oldest building in the Brighton area.'

'That's enough, Jenny, we're beginning to feel like we're in a history lecture,' said Cathy. 'Why don't we go and have another coffee somewhere? We passed a hotel somewhere near here, we could go there. Unless, that is, you have had enough of us for one day?'

'No, of course not, how could I? I'm sorry about the lecture, I did go on, didn't I? I'm a bit of a history freak. I suppose it's doing all that research. Look, I'm free all afternoon, Martin won't be back from his survey until early evening and there's The Black Lion at the bottom of the hill. That must be the one you saw. It will only take us a minute to walk down there.'

'So, you found the missing Vanessa then,' Maddy said as the three of them settled into the leather armchairs in the bar of the hotel.

'What does she look like now? It's been a few years since we've seen her,' said Cathy.

'Very slim, tall, shoulder-length straight hair, probably dyed, quite chatty. She's still working as an athletics coach.'

'She represented Natal, you know, in the inter-province competitions, and would have been accepted for the Olympics, only South Africa was banned from entering from 1964 until 1988 – because of apartheid – so she could only compete in the inter-provinces. She also represented Natal for ice skating. Then she was ill, I can't remember what was wrong, and she gave up competing,' said Maddy.

'That's strange, I loved ice skating too. We used to have a large rink in Brighton; it had a famous ice hockey team, the Brighton Tigers. I used to watch them practise after the Saturday sessions ended, but the rink closed down in the 1970s, I think, and became a cinema and conference complex. She did say she should have sent you her new address after her divorce. But she hasn't lived where she is now for very long, so she probably hasn't got around to it yet. She mentioned she has a daughter, Jackie.'

'Oh, she's divorced, is she?' said Maddy.

'Yes, but not that long ago though.'

'We didn't know that,' continued Maddy. 'Yes, Jacqueline, we haven't seen her either, but it's a bit difficult because, as far as we know, she still lives in South Africa. She must be about thirty by now. Anyway, thank you for that lovely lunch and for showing us around Patcham. We didn't see much of it when we visited you the first time, there was so much to talk about.'

'Look, I'm going to order our coffees,' said Cathy, suddenly standing up.

'I don't expect Vanessa will ever let us know her new address, whatever she said to you about contacting us,' whispered Maddy as Cathy waited at the bar. 'She had an affair with Gerrit soon after they arrived in England. She was always at their house when she wasn't working at her part-time job. It was natural at first, her coming round, as we were the only people they knew. Then, one day, Cathy came home early – she had a part-time evening job to supplement her art sales – feeling unwell. She felt a lot worse when she discovered them *in flagrante* on her bed. Obviously Vanessa's athleticism had extended into the bedroom. As you can imagine, there was a terrible row. Needless to say, we didn't see Vanessa after that. I mean, never your sister's husband. Family's always off-limits. She soon found a job as a coach in Nottingham and Dale, who, as far as we're aware, never knew, told Chris where they had moved to, but Cathy certainly didn't want anything more to do with her, and, well, I could hardly continue to contact her either. I know it takes two, but I'm sure it was Vanessa who made all the running. It took a long time before Gerrit and Cathy were OK again as a couple. Your face, Jenny, what's the matter? Oh God, no, that hasn't happened to you too, has it?'

'No, of course not.'

'Quick, change the subject, she's coming back.'

'Here we go, two coffees.'

'I'll fetch the other one, Cathy.' Jenny jumped up and walked over to the bar and took a deep breath to compose herself, before picking up the remaining coffee and returning to their table.

'You OK, Jenny?' asked Maddy.

'Yes, I'm fine.'

'Don't you feel well?' asked Cathy. 'Look, just because Vanessa doesn't have anything to do with us, that doesn't mean you can't have a relationship with her. After all, she's your sister too.'

'Well, it's early days. I'll see how things go between us. She's a long way away, so it's not so easy to meet up as we three can.'

After hugging and waving goodbye to the twins, Jenny watched as they walked back up Church Hill to where they had left their car. She sat down on the seat by a disused well house that had been built over the Wellesbourne Stream, and looked across the A23 to Patcham Place, a sixteenth-century mansion, reputed to be haunted. She wanted to continue seeing Vanessa; after all, they had more in common than she had with the twins. Also, she could see and feel what Vanessa had meant about them, and she hadn't shared a childhood with them. They were pleased that she had found them and that they were interested in her, but they didn't seem to want or need anyone else, probably because they always had each other. Gerrit had probably felt excluded too, so had easily fallen for Vanessa's advances; that is, if Maddy was right and she had made all the running? But why did Vanessa say that it was Cathy who had an affair with Dale?

22

'I'll start my square over there by the hawthorn.' Jenny pointed into the near distance and started walking away, leaving Martin standing in the car park near Ditchling Nature Reserve.

'It may be too early in the year to see much in the tetrad. Let's do an hour each and then meet back here for coffee,' shouted Martin as she disappeared over the downland ridge. He had recently retired from Natural England, to make way for a younger replacement, and now spent virtually all his spare time as a volunteer for the Sussex Wildlife Trust.

After forty-five minutes of bending over the grassland on her knees, Jenny knelt back, relaxed and stood up looking across at the western ridge of the Downs; in the distance, the shape that was Chanctonbury Ring. It had been dated as a Bronze Age fort and, in 1760, a landowner had planted a ring of beech trees on the banks. The great storm of autumn 1987 had flattened the circle. But it had now grown back to nearly its original height, more ragged, but definitely recognisable. Dark clouds were gathering.

I've had enough, it's too cold, she thought as she turned and walked back up to the car park.

Martin was already removing a rug from the car boot together with a flask. 'I don't know about you, Jenn, but I've had enough for today and I'm gasping for a coffee.'

'We could sit by that bush over there. It should be sheltered from the wind. I'll go and check for thistles.' Martin followed Jenny to a few feet below the South Downs Way, which was today empty of the usual dog walkers and hikers.

'So, how are you getting on with your squares?' said Martin, spreading the tartan rug over the grass.

'It is too early, Martin, especially as it's been a cold, early spring – gorse, of course, dog violets, dandelions, a few cowslips coming into bud and wayfaring trees. We'll have to come back in a few weeks.'

'Same as me. Except I saw the spotted leaves of some early purple orchids. Here's your coffee. I meant to ask you when I came home yesterday, how are you getting on with your new sisters, they came down to the cottage for lunch, didn't they?'

'OK. We had a good time together. I showed them around what's left of the old village and then we walked down to The Black Lion for a coffee.'

'Just OK? That doesn't sound as though you really enjoyed it. Not how it was when you first met them; you were so excited and couldn't stop talking about them. Is the novelty of having siblings wearing off already?'

'No, of course not. We're fine together and love meeting up and talking about our lives. It was different from when they first came to visit us and you were there. It was great, it always is. But we don't have a lot in common.'

'You don't need to have, do you? They're family, not friends. I have absolutely nothing in common with Anna. I never did. Of course, we played together as children, but once we were in our teens, to say our interests diverged would be an understatement. She was into boys, clothes, make-up and music, in that order, and I was into science, the countryside and girls – that includes you, of course.' He grinned, remembering when they had first met at the local youth club. 'Oh, I liked music too, so that was the only thing we had in common. Perhaps if I had a brother, it would have been different, but perhaps not, who knows. Now, we hardly ever talk or see each other. I know she lives in Southampton, but it wouldn't be any different if she lived in Brighton. But she knows I've got her back and I know she'll always be there for me if I need her. That's what families are like, hopefully. You can share interests with friends. Look at us with our shared love of all this.' He circled his arms in the air, embracing the downland and the Weald below them.

'But don't you think some interests are genetic. Because our uncle, you know, the journalist in Cape Town that I told you about, he was interested in natural history, and look at the Curies with their science, and the Leakys with their archaeology. I also read somewhere that religious preferences and even party politics can be inherited.'

'True, I suppose there could be some genetic component, but nurture also plays a large part.'

'I think it's because they're identical twins. I wasn't expecting that. I've never known any before. I feel I always have to meet them as a pair. That makes sense, of course, rather than arranging two separate meetups. It's not like meeting two friends. They seem so close.'

'Yes, I noticed that when we went to Cathy's that time. It was Cathy's, wasn't it? I knew some twins at school but they weren't identical, so they acted and seemed just like normal brother and sister.'

'I've met Vanessa, by the way.'

'Oh God, Jenny, you haven't? I thought you decided to leave it when your letter was returned. When did you meet her then? That's something else you didn't tell me.'

'I didn't tell you because you made it clear you weren't happy about it. So it was easier not to say anything at the time in case it came to nothing. It was towards the end of last year. I've only met her twice, once in Nottingham, then London. She had moved from the address the twins gave me, that's why my letter was returned. The thing is, I like her, and it's easier just meeting and chatting to one person. Better still, we have more in common. She's really into the countryside and the environment as well as her sport. It was Vanessa who mentioned that interests could be genetic. She's an athletics coach and could have made the South African Olympic team if they had been allowed to enter back then. She finds Nottinghamshire boring after South Africa. She told me about the wildlife around Pietermaritzburg – caracals, leopards and hyraxes in the Drakensburg, so I told her the animals and birds we had seen on our trip.'

'Well, yes, but Africa is a bit different to here. You

can't compare the two. Look, I don't mind visiting the twins in Surrey, but I don't fancy driving to Nottingham, so please don't suggest it. Two sisters-in-law are more than enough for me, even if they are identical.'

'By the way, what do you make of Gerrit, Cathy's husband?'

'Seems a solid, steady sort, obviously crazy about Cathy.'

'Well, Cathy's certainly very attractive, a bit more vivacious than Maddy – she's the calmer, quieter twin. I shouldn't think Gerrit would look at anyone else, would you?'

'Gerrit, no, wouldn't have thought so, he's not the type. I can usually tell. Haven't been wrong yet. Why are you asking that?'

'But you did, didn't you? And most people would say you're not the type, whatever that means.'

'Did what?'

'Have an affair, with me.'

'Jenn, that was years ago. It was different with us. We were meant to be together. If I hadn't moved to Southampton with my parents, we would never have parted in the first place. I would never have left Marilyn for anyone but you. Once we met up again, we couldn't let it go, could we?'

'No, we couldn't, but I don't see what years ago has got to do with it. People can have affairs at any age, whatever their "type",' said Jenny as a picture of Izzy flashed into her mind.

'Come here.' Martin pulled Jenny towards him and kissed her long and softly on her lips. Jenny felt her insides melt and knew she would do anything for him. 'Look, I'm pleased you found Vanessa, even though I wasn't keen at first. It's good, that means you can now devote your time to researching for the Trust with me, instead of searching for long-lost family. Anyway, there's no one else to find, hopefully.' He chuckled. 'By the way, I've asked Daniel to come over this evening. He said he'd bring some fish and chips, save us bothering to cook.'

'That's good of him.' Jenny stared into the distance and thought about Nicky's life and how much she would love to be able to say that Nicky was visiting them and bringing fish and chips.

'Are you sure you're OK with that, Jenn?' Martin said, examining her face. 'I can always put him off for another time.'

'No, don't do that.'

23

Summer 2008

'Thanks for phoning, Jenny. You'll be interested to know I managed to visit Rutland Water yesterday. Someone from the club mentioned they were going and asked if I'd like to join them. It's too far otherwise without transport. It's a good place for birdwatching. Ospreys are supposed to nest there, but I didn't see one. Perhaps I was just unlucky,' Vanessa said on one of their frequent phone conversations.

'That reminds me, I found my father's binoculars the other day in our loft. I'd forgotten they were there. They belonged to my grandfather, who was in the First World War. When I was a child, I used to look at the birds in our garden. Not that there was much variety, but being on the edge of the Downs, we used to get our share of finches, chaffinches especially, and house martins used to build their nests under the eaves of the house opposite every summer. But once the farm buildings in the field at the end of our road were demolished, they never returned.'

'That's sad that they don't come back there anymore. Look, I've made a decision, Jenny. I'm going to put this house on the market and look for a place down south. It's been well over a year since I moved here. But I can't settle. I should have moved back south straight after the divorce. I mean, what's keeping me up here? Jackie is busy with her career and her own life; neighbours are non-existent. I'm sure I can find a coaching position wherever I move to, providing it's near a large town.'

'That would be so lovely, if you could. It will be so much easier to meet up and I can show you around. That is, if you're thinking of Sussex.'

'Houses are so much cheaper up here, so I can't afford anywhere near you, and Surrey's even more expensive. Anyway, you wouldn't want me on your doorstep. I was thinking more of the Hastings area, Kent-Sussex border. I've been looking online; it's much cheaper around there. I could afford a flat or, better still, a small, terraced house that's not in a good condition.'

'That's still a lot closer than Nottingham. But how do you feel about leaving your daughter?'

'Oh, she's fine about it, quite excited. Says it will be lovely if I'm near the sea, she can come and visit, so I might actually see more of her.'

'I heard that, Jenn,' said Martin from the sofa as she put the phone down. 'I'm pleased for you. You could meet up more often and it will be a distraction from worrying about Nicky. But, better still, I will never have to visit Nottingham.' He grinned. 'She'll be closer to the twins as well, won't she?'

'Vanessa doesn't have much to do with them. Do

you remember, I told you how she always felt excluded when she was growing up? She said how much she enjoys having a one-to-one relationship with a sister at last.'

*

The sun's rays had turned the loops of the Cuckmere River into a silver ribbon as Jenny left Seaford behind and breached the top of the hill. She drove down into the river valley, rattling over the slats of the narrow wooden bridge that divided the reed beds. She thought how she never tired of this drive between Brighton and Eastbourne. She could have taken the inland route along the A27 – which would have been quicker – but she didn't want to miss the chance of this view. She preferred the bare, windswept Eastern Downs to the homelier wooded slopes of West Sussex. Passing the turn off to Beachy Head, she thought, *another twenty minutes and I should be there.* Whenever she drove this route, which was not often, it seemed as if Eastbourne was creeping ever eastward towards Pevensey Levels. There were new private housing estates and their quota of so-called affordable housing and luxury blocks of flats, interspersed with small trading estates, supermarkets and do-it-yourself stores. Speeding over the straight road that crossed the marshy levels, Jenny turned south towards the sea and climbed into Bexhill. Opposite the railway station, she found the row of brick-built terraced cottages where Vanessa now lived.

'I know it's not a pretty house, not like yours, and only one bedroom. It used to be a railway worker's cottage. Can you believe that parents used to bring up several children in these houses? The old lady I bought it from had lived here for years, hence the terrible '70s wallpaper in every room. I feel I need to put sunglasses on when I'm indoors. But I'll get round to changing it sometime.' Vanessa welcomed Jenny into the tiny hall where steep, wooden, uncarpeted stairs led up to the first floor. 'Once I'm settled, I'll probably extend into the roof to make two bedrooms, that will make it easier for Jackie to come and stay. I decided against a flat. I didn't think I would be happy in one without my own garden. At least this cottage has one; it's narrow and not very long, but I can still sit out there and feel private. The whole place needs work doing, that's why it was cheaper than expected, but all in good time, and I can do a lot of it myself. The thing is, it's really central, which is what I wanted; near the station, beach and some shops.'

'I'm sorry I couldn't help you move,' Jenny said, looking at her red tracksuit and wondering how many she had.

'That's OK. I had some money over after my offer was accepted, so I paid this man with a van to pack and unpack for me. I haven't got much in the way of furniture anyway, and I still have a little left to see me through until I can find a coaching position, I'm hoping for one in Hastings. Also, I'm so excited, did you see that blue car outside? I bought it from a local garage so I can get about. Come on, I'll show you around, it won't take long. Then we can drink a toast to my new house and new life. I've bought some sandwiches – cheese for you, I remembered that's what you prefer – and a home-made sponge cake with buttercream from this bakery down the road. That might be a tiny bit too convenient. I have to watch my weight.'

It was only when Jenny was driving back across Pevensey Levels she remembered that Vanessa had said that her house wasn't a pretty house, not like hers. But Vanessa had never been to her house. She must have described it to her, but she couldn't remember doing so.

24

'Well, this is an improvement on the supermarket café,' said Maddy as she looked around the interior of The Sussex Oak. 'The only problem is, there's no shopping here.'

Jenny thought she much preferred it here. She hated shopping.

'I just love these olde English pubs, they're so cosy. Especially with the oak beams and those brass things. They are horse brasses, aren't they, Jenny?' said Cathy.

'Yes, horse brasses. Lots of pubs have them, from the time when horses were used to pull farm machinery. You must have seen them before, Cathy?'

'I have, but I wasn't quite sure what they're called.'

'I don't know why I didn't suggest meeting here before; it must be exactly halfway between all our houses. I found it on Google and I can't believe I've never been here before, having lived in Sussex all my life,' Jenny said as they made their way to the reserved table by a roaring log fire, even though it was July. She thought that, now they had met several times, they were completely at ease in each other's company; at least, she was, and hoped they were too…

'That's often the way though, isn't it,' said Maddy. 'When we lived in Cape Town, we only ever visited Cape Point or went up Table Mountain when family or friends came to visit.'

'Another advantage, we can have alcohol here.' Cathy laughed. 'Are you having your usual, Maddy?' Not waiting for her reply, she asked, 'What about you, Jenny?'

'White wine spritzer, please.' She pulled the oak table towards her to enable them to sit in line with the fire. 'Maddy, I wanted to tell you, while Cathy's at the bar, that Vanessa has recently moved to Sussex. She's bought a tiny, terraced house in Bexhill.'

'Why has she moved? What about her job?'

'She couldn't settle in her new house after her divorce. It was on one of those new estates that are deserted during the day, and she missed her old neighbours. She gave it well over a year to get used to it. She said everybody was always so busy, either working or they had young families, so she found it lonely when she wasn't working, which was often during the daytime. She also mentioned the countryside isn't so interesting up there as down this way. It's very flat around Nottingham and definitely not as varied as here in the south.'

'I didn't think she was that interested in the countryside. She certainly wasn't in Surrey and we lived near Box Hill and the North Downs. Mind you, that's a bit unfair of me to say that, as she was only getting adjusted to living here in England then I suppose. She's nearer to you now, isn't she?'

'Yes, but not that near, she needs to be near a large town for work.'

'Did you say Bexhill? Where's that?'

'It's over near Hastings, quite near Kent.'

'At least she hasn't moved back to Surrey.'

'She couldn't afford to, Maddy. She had to look at houses or flats in the Hastings area. She could have looked in East Kent, but that was too far away. I thought you ought to know, being family, but I didn't want to mention it in front of Cathy. I did say to her what about her daughter, won't she miss her if she moves further away?'

'Well, Bexhill's no further from South Africa than Nottingham is, Jenny. As far as I know, Jackie, her daughter, is still in Johannesburg, at least she was the last I heard from her. She's an accountant, works for one of the big international firms. I was quite close to her years ago, and we still exchange Xmas cards, the last one I had was two years ago. Vanessa told us she was always good at maths, like herself. Good job someone is. We're not. She must have moved or transferred to England because her parents are here.'

'Yes, I suppose she must have.'

'Suppose who must have? What am I missing?' Cathy said as she placed two drinks on the table. 'Tell me in a sec. I'll just get the lager.'

'We were only talking about Lorna, my daughter,' said Jenny, picking up one of the menus. 'Let's decide what we're eating.'

'I looked at one on the bar. There's a good choice. I'm having the chilli, the spicier the better, like life.' Cathy laughed as she sat down next to Jenny.

'Your life is hot enough from what you told me on the way here.'

'What's this?' asked Jenny.

'Cathy fancies her new boss at her job in the car showrooms.'

'You would too if you saw him. He's not the slightest bit interested in art, but what's that got to do with it? I don't plan on taking him to the National Gallery. Unfortunately, he doesn't seem to know I exist. I'm too old for him probably. But wait 'til Christmas. I'm going on the hunt for some mistletoe for our work's Xmas party. From what I've heard, they are *something else.* If you get my drift. I'll wait 'til he's had a few drinks, then I'll pounce.' She laughed.

Jenny smiled at her sister. She could certainly imagine her having an affair with someone, but why would Maddy say it was Vanessa who had an affair with Gerrit? Perhaps that was what Cathy had told her and, being her twin, she had never questioned it. She loved to hear Cathy speak in her broad South African accent. It was much stronger than Maddy's, which had softened by the years she had lived in England.

Two hours later, the three sisters wandered through the village, trying to peer inside the old cottages that lined the high street. Arriving at the church, they walked under the ancient yew tree, its branches forming a porch over the lychgate into the churchyard. Jenny remembered reading, the evening before, that besides the poet William Cowper's ancestors having lived here, Percy Shelley had been born and spent his early years at Field Place just outside the village. 'Hail to thee blithe spirit! Bird thou never wert...' she muttered to herself as she heard the song of a skylark – immortalised in Shelley's poem – singing in her mind as they wandered around the churchyard. Later, as she drove home past Shipley, a few miles to the south, she recalled that another poet, Hilaire Belloc, had also wandered along these lanes and, inspired by the countryside, had composed Jenny's favourite poem, *The South Country*. Seeing the blunt hills that lay ahead of her, she muttered the lines she had memorised as a child, 'The great hills of the South Country. They stand against the sea; And it's there walking in the high woods. That I could wish to be, And the men that were boys when I was a boy walking along with me…' and wondered once more why she had never driven around here before. Perhaps she could bring Vanessa here once she had settled in her house.

25

'Washed Ashore.' Vanessa read out the words scratched into the small wooden cross that headed the grass mound in Friston Churchyard.

'Yes, I saw this the first time I came here. No name, so presumably no identification papers or disc. If he had any, they must have been lost at sea.'

'Do you know, Jenny, I'm so pleased I moved down here. There's so much more variation in the countryside here than Nottingham, and I love being by the sea. Dale and I did go once to Skegness. The beaches were sandy, but it was bitterly cold on that North Sea coast. It was winter though.'

'Yes, I'm pleased you moved too. I'm enjoying showing you around. I'm revisiting places I haven't seen for years. It's always the way, isn't it? You don't often visit places when you live nearby?'

'The views over the Downs are fantastic.'

'They are, but we better start walking if we're going to make Birling Gap for lunch.' Jenny turned and walked towards the Tapsel gate that swivelled on its central post as she gave it a push. 'I think this is my favourite village pond, Vanessa,' Jenny said as they stood and stared at the yellow water lilies that covered the pond in front of the churchyard.

'Well, it must take some beating, especially at this time of year. I love the yellow flowers; I've never seen those before.'

'I don't remember seeing them here before either. It must have been a different time of year.' Jenny remembered that it was near here, in the Cuckmere Valley, where she and Martin had started their affair. She smiled as she recalled the first time they had made love in his office at the Visitors' Centre. It was one evening after they had driven to the shingle beach at the mouth of the river. It was as clear as if it had been yesterday.

'What are you smiling at?' Vanessa's eyes twinkled in the sunlight.

'A memory of myself and Martin.'

'Tell me more; it must be a good one.'

'It is. I'm sorry he wasn't around the other week when you came over. We'll arrange another lunch date, and I'll make sure he's at home next time. We'd better go.'

The two women walked down the chalk track towards Crowlink and, about a mile further on, reached the South Downs Way. They walked eastwards on the springy turf that spread inland from the Seven Sister cliffs. 'Don't get too close to the edge, Vanessa,' Jenny shouted as Vanessa suddenly ran over to the barbed wire fence that stood two metres back from the cliff edge. Vanessa bent down, flattening herself in order to wriggle under the barbed wire, then, laying on her stomach, started to take photos, the strong breeze blowing her hair across her face.

'It's dangerously deceptive here, because of the chalk overhangs.' Jenny shouted to make her voice heard above the wind as she ran over towards the wire.

'I think I can see the lighthouse at Beachy Head. I must take a photo of you here, Jenny. It's perfect with the position of the sun now. Didn't I tell you I like to live life on the edge?'

'Well, let me take one of you too then, but please come back away from the edge, Vanessa, you're making me really nervous,' Jenny shouted.

'Don't worry, I'm fine. I must take one more, then I'm coming back. Can you walk along the shore at the bottom of these cliffs? I'd love to do that sometime,' Vanessa asked as she squeezed back under the wire that snagged her grey tracksuit top and, standing up, handed Jenny her camera. 'Here looks good, with the cliffs in the background, Jenny.'

'Yes, you can, but it's risky; you would have to ensure the tide was going out before you set off. There are always reports of people having to be rescued by the coastguard. There's no way up until you reach Birling Gap. Or else back the other way to Cuckmere Haven.'

'We'll leave that 'til another time then. How much longer until we reach our lunch stop? These steep hills are killing my legs, I'm not used to them.'

'I thought you were the athlete.' Jenny grinned. 'Just this next bit, then according to my map it's all downhill to the café. Give me your camera again and I'll take another photo of you with the hill in the background.'

*

'I really enjoyed our walk today,' said Jenny later as they sat side by side on the grassy bank and leaned against the churchyard wall. They were each eating a slice of buttered tea loaf and looking across the path at the pond.

'Me too, although I'm not used to all that walking up and down steep hills. As you know, it's pretty flat around Nottingham, my legs have had a good workout though and I expect my muscles will ache tomorrow. Thanks for bringing the cake by the way.'

'That's OK. It will keep us going until we get home.'

'Jenny.'

'Yes,'

'I've a confession to make.'

'You do?'

'Yes, it wasn't Cathy who had an affair with Dale. She wouldn't have done that to her younger sister. I'm not saying she wouldn't have an affair with anyone, she probably would; in fact, I'm sure she has, but not with her brother-in-law. It was me that had an affair with Gerrit. It was unforgivable and I feel ashamed. I suppose, in some subconscious way, I wanted to get back at them for always excluding me. He's an attractive man, though, and I was bored and lonely when we first came here. I know that's no excuse. Mind you, he didn't take much persuading.'

'Oh, Vanessa, you didn't have to tell me this.'

'I did. I lied about it before because I wanted you to feel sorry for me. I was frightened you wouldn't want to see me again once you'd met the twins, especially as I lived further away. I don't expect that you would ever do that, would you?'

'What, have an affair? Well, as I told you, Martin and I were both married to other people when we met up again. So, yes, I have had an affair, same as you, we even left our marriages to be with each other.'

'No, not have an affair. These things happen, and yours wasn't with your brother-in-law, was it? I mean deliberately tell someone a lie about what really happened.'

Jenny's heart bounced against the wall of her chest as she continued to stare at the pond while deciding whether or not to continue. 'No, I have.'

'You have! My God, Jenn,' Vanessa turned her head and smiled, 'I was feeling so bad that I told you it was Cathy.'

'I've lied by omission.'

'What do you mean?'

'I haven't told Martin the truth.'

'Truth about what? You haven't had an affair since being with Martin, have you? You're so happy together. I know when a marriage is unhappy, believe me.'

'Yes, we are happy together, that's why I haven't told Martin the truth. I never can.'

'Haven't told him what, Jenny? Are you seriously ill?' Vanessa stared at Jenny, a concerned look on her face.

Jenny's heart pounded in her ears and her breathing became shallow as she hesitated to go on, wishing that Vanessa had never mentioned that she had lied. 'That he's my half-brother.'

'What?'

'Yes, he's my half-brother, but he'll never know because I can't tell him and I never will. You see, we weren't brought up together. His mother – she's dead, by the way

– is my birth mother, she had a short affair with Gordon – our father – when he was re-cooperating in Hove in 1945, after being released from the POW camp. Martin's father, Enrico, was away serving in the British Air Force, and I was adopted as a baby, so he, Enrico, never knew his wife had an affair while he was away and a child. But I didn't find that out until Martin and I had left our marriages to live together. I was so happy at that time that I decided I was strong enough to find my roots. Martin's mother's name is on my original birth certificate, which only I can ever apply for and see. There's a blank where my birth father's name would normally be. If the father doesn't come to the registration, his name is omitted. Gordon would have been repatriated to South Africa and reunited with his wife and Andrew when my mother gave birth to me. Once I read it – the certificate – I burnt it. So, you see, I couldn't tell him, it was too late then anyway. How could I break up with him, when we had already brought so much hurt upon our families by deciding to be together? We were so attracted to each other, even as teenagers. We lived in the same town but not near each other, and we met at a youth club near where he lived. I realised, when I knew the truth, that was the reason why his family moved to Southampton. His/my mother recognised me as the daughter she had adopted when I went to their house on his sister Anna's birthday. She asked my birthday, so I told her. I remember she then dropped a tray of fairy cakes. I remember it as if it were yesterday. They scattered all over the floor and I helped her pick them up. They moved a few weeks later. Genetic sexual attraction, that's what it's called, when you're attracted to a family member you haven't been brought up with. I hardly ever think about it now, it's been so many years that we've lived together, built a life together.' Jenny's voice trembled as she spoke. 'You're the shocked one now, aren't you?'

Vanessa stared at Jenny. 'Yes, I am.'

'Perhaps I should never have told you. You are the only person I've ever told. I haven't even told Gail, my oldest and best friend. I suppose I wanted to make you feel better about lying and blaming someone else.'

'No, I'm pleased you have. I'm just amazed that something like that could happen. I don't blame you. You didn't know who he was when you met up with each other again and started living together. Supposing he finds out though?' Vanessa stared open-mouthed at Jenny.

'He never can. I'm the only person who has access to my adoption file and my original birth certificate. I started to search for my birth mother once we had been together a couple of years; Martin was pleased that I was doing it. Once I had seen my birth certificate with his mother's name written in black and white as my mother, I was in shock; I couldn't believe it, I didn't want to believe it. So, I burnt it immediately and told Martin that I didn't keep my appointment with the social worker because I felt ill and wasn't ready to have the information after all. So, Ricco, her husband, was demobbed later in 1946, came home to his wife and Martin, none the wiser that his wife had an affair and a child while he was away. They then had Anna, Martin's sister. My birth mother died several years ago now, so Martin will never find out.'

'You're shaking, come here.' Vanessa pulled Jenny

towards her. 'You say in all this time you've never told anyone else?'

'No, who could I tell? Not my children. I'd just left Rob, their father, to be with Martin. As I said, Gail's my oldest friend, she was the only person, until now, whom I could have told. But I just couldn't, it's too big a revelation. I probably wouldn't even have told you. I didn't think when I woke up, oh, I'll tell Vanessa today as she's my sister. It was just in the moment. I suppose I wanted to make you feel better about yourself and lying to me. Or perhaps it is because I did need to tell someone after all these years.'

'Are you going to tell the twins too?'

'God no, there is no reason to.'

'Hang on, suppose someone else, like Martin's son or sister, do a DNA test. They would then know that you're their relation, wouldn't they?'

'Daniel would never do that, neither would Anna, they have no reason to. Anyway, neither of them is interested in family history,' Jenny said quickly.

'But surely, once you knew the truth, didn't that change how you felt about Martin? It must have affected your relationship. You know, the physical side?'

'It did for a while, of course, I couldn't get it out of my head. Martin kept asking me what was wrong. I just said it was about work, I'd decided to study about that time for some legal executive exams, to take my mind off it, and I was having problems with Rob and my children then too – you know, due to the divorce – so he left it at that. He wanted me so much physically back then that once he started making love to me, I couldn't help but respond, so after a while, that carried on as normal. We hadn't grown up together, you see, so when we met again, we were strangers, apart from those few weeks when we went out together as teenagers. The years went by, life happened. It receded so much into the background it was almost forgotten. It didn't seem important after a while and doesn't now. I hardly ever think about it. I'm still trembling now though through talking about it to you because I never have.'

'Well, don't drive back yet, it's better to be late and safe, than on time and dead.' Vanessa smiled. 'I can't lose you so soon after meeting you.'

'Look, let's make a date when you can come over for lunch and meet Martin. We don't look alike. He's got the Italian looks of his father, while I resemble our father, don't I? I'm a bit similar to my birth mother in colouring and body shape. Martin had a photo of her, which I tucked away somewhere so I don't have to see it.'

'I know you said Martin will never be able to find out, but suppose he does a DNA test? They're becoming much more common now,' Vanessa said, standing up and brushing the grass from her clothes.

'Why would he? He knows who he is. He was close to both his parents. He always says Anna, his sister, is enough family for him. Mind you, she can be a pain. He's not interested in family matters, apart from myself, Lorna, Nicky and Daniel, his son. They're more than enough family for him. So that will never happen. Pull me up, please, my legs are like jelly.' Jenny reached for Vanessa's hand. 'Look, why don't you come over, say, two weeks next Monday. Martin's always home on a Monday. If that's OK with you? Oh, no, I've just realised I've got the dentist that afternoon. It will have to be the following week, so three weeks next Monday. I'll phone you if there's a problem.' They wandered across the grass to where they had parked their cars hours earlier.

'That sounds fine, Jenny. But are you sure you'll be OK driving back?'

'Look, you go, Vanessa. I'll sit in the car for a while, to make sure.'

'Well, call me when you get home then, otherwise I'll worry.'

26

Beyond the tower blocks and cranes of the city, the Channel glistened in the late-morning sun. Jenny quickened her pace as she retraced her steps along the chalk track, thinking she must tell Martin about the lone raven she had seen flying above the ridge of the Downs. An unmistakable honking sound had made her stop and look up and watch it as it flew eastwards. They had heard that a pair were now nesting in the chalk quarry at Lewes. Earlier that morning, she had walked north from Patcham along the track to the Chattri, a marble memorial dedicated to the Indian soldiers who died fighting for Britain in the First World War. Any injured soldiers were treated in a temporary hospital in The Royal Pavilion, and the Hindu and Sikh soldiers who died were cremated at the Chattri. After reading the inscription on the stone, she continued walking northwards. She wished Vanessa could be with her as she always felt vulnerable on her own if there were not many people about. Not that she thought that every man she came across was a potential rapist. But she always had in her mind stories carried in the national papers of some lone woman being attacked for no reason. So, she was always wary and kept her car keys in her pocket. She resented the fact that Martin could wander about wherever he wanted free of these concerns, while for herself – in fact, since she had been a child – that was always something to be considered and limiting as to where she could walk. Reaching the South Downs Way, she had stopped for her flask of coffee and recalled a recent conversation with Maureen. She had grown tired of stalking her daughter and had asked an intermediary to write to her letting her know that she was interested in meeting her, or at least would like to receive a letter from her. Unfortunately, the intermediary had to impart the sad news to Maureen that her daughter had no interest in either meeting up or corresponding with her. So, Jenny had tried to comfort a tearful Maureen on the phone by saying that this response was not uncommon – she had known it happen once before, and then later the adoptee changed their mind – and that her daughter would hopefully change her mind too at some future date, so she shouldn't give up hope completely.

Jenny reached the Brighton bypass that now sliced through fields that had once belonged to Patcham Court Farm, where a horse and a donkey used to graze. She walked over the road bridge that crossed the A27 towards the old farmhouse. At the top of Church Hill, she stopped. A blue car was parked outside their house. *That looks like Vanessa's car*, she thought and, reading the number plate, recognised the first letters. *It is hers, what's she doing here? It's not today she's coming to lunch.* She turned and walked around the corner, standing behind the flint wall that surrounded the converted tithe barn and waited.

Fifteen minutes passed until she saw her front door open and stared as a flash of pale blue from a summer dress lit up the front step as Vanessa hesitated and then walked across the road, followed by Martin. He accompanied her to her car, waited while she settled herself into the driver's seat, closed the door, and waved her off as she drove down Church Hill. Jenny stood for a few minutes then walked along the road for about one hundred metres before turning around and going down to their cottage, wondering what it was that had made her hesitate about going home when she knew that Vanessa was there, and decided it was embarrassment.

'The kettle has just boiled if you want a drink?' Martin turned from the sink where he was washing up two mugs as Jenny walked through their lounge. 'You'll never guess who I've just met, and you've just missed?'

'Well, you'd better tell me then.' Jenny sat down on the sofa and although pleased that he was telling her, her heart beat faster, as she remembered what she had told Vanessa.

'Vanessa, your sister.'

'What, she's been here? Why? It's next Monday she's coming for lunch?'

'I know, but she thought it was today. In fact, you've only just missed her by about ten minutes.'

'That's a shame. I did mention today, but then I changed it to next Monday because of the dentist this afternoon.'

'Yes, she remembered once I mentioned your appointment. She said she felt a right idiot and when I told her you weren't here, she was going to go straight home. But I insisted she come in and have a coffee first. I can see the family resemblance around the mouth. She's very attractive. She certainly made an effort to look good, and all for nothing.'

'Had she? That's good, but it wasn't all for nothing, was it? She met you. I haven't got time to call her until after my appointment and she's not back in Bexhill yet, anyway. I'd better grab some lunch, otherwise I'll be late. The thing is, I wanted to be here when she came, so I could introduce you to her properly.'

'Well, you still can, next Monday.'

'It's not quite the same, is it? You've already met her. How long was she here?'

'Oh, I don't know, I was on the second floor at my computer when I heard the bell. About half an hour, I suppose.'

'Did she say anything about our walk to Birling Gap?'

'No, why would she? She was embarrassed about her mistake.'

'Look, I'd better go or I'll be late.' Jenny grabbed a sausage roll and banana from the fridge and left, realising she hadn't told Martin about the raven.

Vanessa's name flashed up on Jenny's phone as she walked towards her car. She was going to ignore it but changed her mind.

'Jenny, I'm such an idiot. I thought it was today I was coming to lunch. Martin said you were out and told me about your appointment, then, of course, the penny dropped; it's next Monday, isn't it? I don't usually get my dates muddled but it was a bit dramatic when we last met, wasn't it? I suppose I didn't take it in.'

137

'Yes, it was. It must have been a shock when I told you. I'm sorry you had a wasted journey. It's partly my fault, I should have sent you a text to confirm the date when I'd got home. I did mention today, didn't I? Then I remembered I had the dentist.'

'Yes, you did. Hope it's nothing too painful. I hate going. It's almost a phobia.'

'No, just a filling.'

'Anyway, I'm on my way home. I'm at Lewes and just stopped off for a walk by the river, it's such a nice day. I remember you said ravens are nesting in the chalk quarry, so that's where I am, not that I've seen them yet. It seemed a waste of a warm day to go straight home. Martin's so lovely, Jenny, I see what you mean about looking like his Italian father. I expect he told you that I was going to go straight back once I realised my mistake, but he insisted that I come in and have a coffee, even though he was in the middle of some article he's writing. I felt such an idiot. Please tell him I'm sorry I disturbed him. Good news, by the way, I've been offered and accepted the job at Hastings Athletic Club.'

'Yes, I'll tell him. So, we'll see you next Monday about twelve-thirty then.'

'Yes, I'll look forward to meeting Martin properly then.'

Jenny ended the call, thinking that it sounded like she already had, and as she opened her car door, she thought, *why on earth did I tell Vanessa about Martin?*

27

September 2008

'I've been thinking of coming back here for years, and at last I've made it. But everything is so much smaller than I thought it was. Do you think it's always the same when you come back as an adult, to somewhere you remember from your childhood?' Jenny asked as they wandered along a lane in Guernsey.

'Yes, probably, but maybe it's because we were smaller then. Although when I went back to where we lived in Southampton, I didn't notice it, but I was a teenager when we lived there.'

'This lane used to be lined with greenhouses crammed full of tomatoes; now there are just bungalows. I remember one morning we were passing and the owner gave us each a tomato to try. It was the best I had ever tasted. This lane seemed so much longer too back then. Look, we've nearly reached Vazon Bay. Dad and I used to take Mrs Sebire's two Labradors, one black and one golden, for their run on the sand before breakfast. That was the highlight of the holiday for me. We came here three years running, always staying at the same guest house. I didn't expect it still to be a guest house, not after all these years, but even though it's been converted into a shop and post office, the exterior of the house still looks the same as it does in the photo I showed you.'

'That's unusual that you came here for a holiday in the 1950s, Jenn, especially flying here. We didn't go anywhere much until the 1960s. Before then, we only had days out. Even when we did go away, we only stayed in a caravan in Dorset, so not exactly far away, and after that, I was too old to want to go anywhere with my parents.'

'Yes, I remember boasting to my friends at junior school that we were going on holiday in an aeroplane; I was the first to fly anywhere, nobody else we knew had. Mind you, the first time, we came over by boat from Southampton. We wouldn't have gone away at all if our doctor hadn't insisted that my mother needed a break. She'd had two serious stomach operations and somebody Dad knew, probably from work, mentioned that here would be ideal as it's quieter than Jersey. Dad would never have found it on his own. It was easier for him to go on someone's recommendation. I often thought that if someone had suggested Greenland, we would have gone there. It was ideal for us here though, quiet, so he was right about that, and I remember we had lovely food at the guest house and plenty of it. We even had crab salad.'

'Well now we're here, shall we walk along the bay? The sea's such a lovely blue with the sun shining. It might be windy though.'

'We must. I used to walk to Grandes Rocques, that's the next bay along, while my parents relaxed on this beach. There's a large rock in the shape of a lion and I remember clambering over the rocks to reach it. Then there were the rock pools to investigate with my net, plenty of small crabs. I must have been gone for quite a time, but I can't remember my parents ever worrying about me. I'm sure I learnt to swim here too; no pebbles and the water's so shallow. I have a photo of me with one of those rubber rings around my middle. Let's see how long it takes us to reach the next bay.'

The sea lapped the hard, wet shore scattered with multicoloured, splintered shells, while a few metres back soft, golden sand stretched to mini dunes and marram grass that banked up against the sea wall.

'I don't expect I'll find any ormer shells here now. Not after what that fisherman said yesterday. I can't believe how scarce they've become, and that he can only collect them for twenty days a year. I used to find so many here, large and small ones. I still have some at home. They have the most beautiful mother-of-pearl lining. I'll show you them when we get back.'

'It's the way of the world now, Jenn. So many species endangered, not just mammals. I think they're related to abalone, which are quite a delicacy, so probably they've been overfished. By the way, what did Vanessa want yesterday? It was her on the phone, wasn't it?'

'Only to wish us a good trip and to say that she's looking forward to hearing all about it when we get back. Obviously, she's never been here. I have the feeling she'd like to come sometime.' Jenny brushed her hair away from her face. 'It's a strong wind here for early September.'

'We're exposed to the westerlies just here. Perhaps she could come with you then, another time?'

'Maybe, but it's a big step going away on holiday with someone you haven't known for very long. It can be difficult with someone you think you know well. On the other hand, it's brought back so many memories coming back here and I'm really enjoying sharing them with you. So, I'm sure she'd be interested in coming here. I'll think about it. Look, I can't stand this wind and it's cold now that the sun's gone in, let's go inland. We could make for that bunker.'

Martin was peering out to sea shading his eyes from the sun with his hand. 'I've just seen a gannet. You won't see it, it's under the water now. But look where I'm pointing, just to the right of those rocks, and you'll probably see another one dive.'

Martin turned and started walking in the soft sand towards the concrete bunker, leaving Jenny by the shoreline shading her eyes and peering out to sea. After a minute she turned and ran up the sand towards Martin, linking her arm in his. 'It's too windy to stay down there. I didn't see one.'

'There's always tomorrow. We have one more day, so hopefully, if that wind dies down, we could come back here and walk to the next bay then. I didn't realise there were German bunkers on the island. I should have, because I know the Channel Islands were occupied. It makes sense though. We're on the north-west side of the island. They would have had a good view of the Channel and any invasion from here.'

'We can go down into it. I used to explore them. I remember this one being cold, damp and smelly. There was German writing on the inside walls, probably swear words. I was too young to realise at the time, but anti-

German feelings must still have run high here then. It was only ten years after the end of the war.' A memory flashed through Jenny's mind as she spoke. 'I remember, one day we were at the guest house and I was sitting on the stairs, probably waiting for dinner, when I saw Mr Sebire pull his shirt up over his shoulders to show my father red weals across his back where he had been beaten by German guards. My father told my mother later that he'd been interned in a forced-labour camp on Alderney and had been starved and beaten. I don't know why he'd been sent there, probably resisting the occupation. I read a while ago that there had been a slave-labour camp on Alderney, which had held prisoners of war from Russia. They were treated the worst of all, because the Soviet Union hadn't signed the Geneva Convention. I thought of Mr Sebire when I read that, but he wasn't Russian, so perhaps he was in a different camp,' Jenny said as she followed Martin down uneven concrete steps into the bunker.

'Yes, I think there was a programme on TV about Alderney. Look, Jenn, the German writing is still on this wall here along with other graffiti.'

'So it is, a real blast from the past, and it's still damp and smelly down here. It's too windy to walk any further along the beach, so what do you say about driving back to St Peter Port? It should be sheltered on that side of the island. We can go for a walk, or we could just go back to the hotel and make the most of a free afternoon. What do you think?' Jenny smiled at Martin while wrapping her arm around his waist.

'I think your second suggestion is the best one.' He smiled.

28

'I think I'll have a ploughman's with cheese, not ham. I've eaten enough meat this week already and I'm trying to cut back on processed food, after reading that article in yesterday's paper.'

It was a warm, still September afternoon and they had just completed surveying the final part of the reserve that they had started in the spring. They then drove down the steep, winding road under the Beacon, which was the nearest Sussex came to a mountain road, to the village of Ditchling.

'I'll join you with that then; if you go and find a table, I'll order. I've got something to tell you that you'll be interested in.'

Jenny found a table that still caught the rays of the sun and relaxed as she watched a man walk a bulldog past the cottages in the village street and thought how much she loved seeing that breed of dog; they seemed to have so much character. She wondered whether they should consider having another dog, not a bulldog, but a mongrel like Toby. She assumed Martin wanted to talk about Daniel, as he had driven over to see him in Lewes earlier that day. Daniel was always coming up with ideas, usually about quitting his job to become self-employed, but recently had toyed with the idea of moving his family abroad for a new life, not that his current one needed any improvement. Jenny thought they had everything a couple could possibly want. A new detached house near the centre of Lewes with a view of the castle, good local schools for their two children, a wife willing to work, not like Marilyn. *She certainly wouldn't be happy if her only son and grandchildren moved abroad,* Jenny thought. But, if they did, she might, perhaps, stop comparing Daniel's life with Nicky, who seemed doomed to spend the rest of his in supported accommodation without a partner or the children she knew he wanted. Sometimes she wondered, but then hated herself for thinking it, whether it would be easier for her if Nicky could move abroad, but then that was never going to happen.

'They only had one cheese, so I'll have the ham,' Martin said as he placed their drinks on the wooden table. 'They're bringing the food in about ten minutes. Good, glad to see we've still got some sun here.'

'So, what was it you wanted to tell me?'

'Well, when I was at Daniel's earlier, I spoke to Anna on the phone.'

'Oh, that hardly ever happens.'

'Exactly, only when she wants something. She phoned Daniel, not sure why, though it could have been because of his birthday last week, which she probably forgot, but when he told her I was there, she asked to speak to me too.'

'Actually, I like Anna. She's fun and there's something

uncomplicatedly selfish about her, and she does visit us from time to time.'

'True, but only when she's in the area. She doesn't put herself out to come over. In fact, she doesn't put herself out for anything or anyone unless it's something she wants or needs. She always was spoilt. I blame Papa – his little princess. Anyway, you'll never guess what she said?' Not waiting for Jenny's reply, he continued, 'She asked me if she could have the name of that ancestry website that you used to find your…'

Jenny knew Martin was carrying on speaking, but his words were muffled, her ears were filled with cotton wool. She stared across the road looking but not seeing the man with the bulldog returning from his walk. She felt the blood drain from her face. She then turned to Martin.

'Jenny, what on earth's the matter? Your face has changed colour. Are you OK? Did you hear what I just said?'

'Anna wants the ancestry website. Why?' Her voice trembled.

'Well, now she's a grandmother, she wants to find out more about our Italian ancestors. I can only go back as far as my grandparents and my dad's cousin when they came over here before the First World War. I don't know anything about the family they left behind in Italy. Also, with Ricco and his elder brother dead, there's no one alive over here now who could tell her anything.'

'She doesn't want to do a DNA test then?' Jenny could hardly speak the words as her heart rate had doubled and her ears pounded. She remembered Vanessa words about the possibility of a member of Martin's family doing a DNA test, and she had dismissed the possibility out of hand.

'Your voice sounds really strange, Jenn. Not as far as I know. I told her that she can just put what she knows of our family tree on the site, and hopefully some Italian relations might respond with more information about them. I remember you telling me that is what one of the twins did, and how it helped you find your father, that's right, isn't it? They didn't do a DNA test, did they?'

'No, they didn't. It was Maddy who put the family tree on the site. She didn't need to do a test. She didn't need to because she knew who her family were. So, Anna doesn't need to either. It's cheaper if you don't.' Jenny felt her heartbeat gradually slowing as she spoke.

'OK, well perhaps you could phone her and tell her that sometime then. There's no rush. I'm just amazed that she's suddenly become interested in genealogy; she was never into any kind of research, only about clothes and make-up. You still look terrible, Jenn, do you feel OK?'

'No, I feel a bit sick. I'm not sure if I can eat anything after all.'

'Well, here she comes with our food.'

'I think I'll just go for a walk. Look, you start. I'll see how I feel when I come back. It won't get cold, will it?' Jenny stood up, grabbed her bag and left the table, feeling Martin's eyes following her as she walked on shaky legs out of the pub garden. She turned left along the village street for a few metres until she came to a wooden seat. Checking she was out of sight from Martin, she sat down and removed her mobile phone from her bag. She took a few deep breaths in and slowly out until she felt calm enough to find Anna's number. It rang for a few seconds before she heard Anna's voice. 'Hi, Anna, it's Jenny. I'm glad you're there. I hear you want the details of the ancestry website that I used. Yes, I know I didn't have to let you know this quick but I've got the time to speak now. I'm a bit busy the rest of this week. There are a few sites, you know, but not all are good ones. Martin told me you were interested in finding your Italian ancestors, is that right? OK, so you don't need to do a DNA test, you do know that, don't you? It makes it much more expensive if you do that. I only did one because I didn't have my family's name, whereas you do. Oh good, then just put the names you know on a family tree on the site then, it's easy to do. I'll e-mail you with the name of the site and I'll get Martin to put in the e-mail everything he knows about your family. So, just to be clear, you don't need to waste your money doing a DNA test, just put the names of your relations on the site and I'm sure you'll get some replies. Thank you, I'll tell him. We'll see you some time then, oh, and congratulations on becoming a grandmother at last, it's been a long wait, we're very pleased for you, bye.' Jenny sat holding her phone for several minutes while her heart gradually slowed to its normal rate and thinking that she would e-mail Anna tomorrow with the name of a different ancestry company from the one she had used. She had looked at the site herself and dismissed it as not as good as the one she eventually decided to join. Knowing Anna, her interest in genealogy would be a 'flash in the pan'. She would soon forget all about it and move on to more interesting things, like fussing over her new granddaughter. After taking a few more deep breaths, she stood up and began walking slowly back along the road to the garden and Martin.

29

2009

Spring was late. The burgeoning leaves on the trees were reluctant to face the north-east wind, that had blown for the past ten days. Jenny wrapped her scarf tighter around her neck as she walked along the path that ran alongside the chalk stream. The strong April sun had disappeared behind a cloud, forcing Jenny to retrace her steps to where she had left her car. She thought back over the last few weeks. Vanessa had told her in February that she had booked to go on holiday to Guernsey for five days with her daughter in May. But on Monday evening she had phoned to say her daughter was unable to go because of work commitments.

'You will come with me, won't you, Jenny? I know it's not what was planned, and you've been there recently, but I don't want to miss this chance. It sounded so idyllic, and you can show me around. It will be so good if you can. You've got to see what Martin thinks, but it's only five days, so surely he can't object to that?'

'I can't say for sure this minute, Vanessa. I'll mention it to Martin and call you later this week.'

Jenny sat in her car staring at the bank of celandines. They were at least three weeks later than usual this year and some were still in bloom. To her, they were always the first sign of spring. She was thinking of the best way to broach the subject of going away with Vanessa. When they were in Guernsey, it was Martin who had mentioned the possibility of her visiting the island with her, and it was her who wasn't keen on the idea, so perhaps he wouldn't mind too much after all. She would have to speak to him that evening. She had been reluctant to mention the possibility of going away with Vanessa before, because she had spent so much time with her since she had moved to Sussex, and Martin, who hardly ever objected to anything she did, had been making noises to the effect that they had hardly been out together for months. Their trip to Guernsey last September was the last time they had been away, and due to the early onset and length of winter, days out this year had been few and far between. Jenny had placated him, saying it was only the first year that Vanessa was living down here, so he shouldn't begrudge the time she had spent with her, adding that it's not easy for anyone to make new friends when you're not young anymore.

'Well, she's very attractive, and she's not old. I would think she would attract friends of both sexes very easily.'

'Do you find her attractive then?'

'Well, she is your sister, and you do look a bit alike.' Martin had chuckled. 'Take it as a compliment.'

The fact that Martin found Vanessa attractive silenced Jenny. Brought up as an only child, she had no experience of sibling rivalry. It hadn't entered her head until then that Martin could even think of Vanessa as attractive. She was just her sister. 'Do you fancy her then?'

Martin put his head on one side as he always did when puzzled by Jenny's response. 'For God's sake, Jenny, what sort of question's that?'

'It's the sort of question any woman would ask when a man says that he finds another woman attractive.'

'It might surprise you to know that in the past I've found a lot of women attractive, but it doesn't mean I'm going to leap into bed with them.'

'You might have done if they had made themselves available.' Jenny thought about Vanessa's affair with Gerrit, and her own jealously of Izzy.

'But they didn't, and neither will Vanessa. She's your sister, for God's sake. Can we change the subject?'

'Izzy's available though, and has been for quite a while, hasn't she?' Jenny couldn't help voicing what she had always, until now, left unsaid. She watched his expression and waited for his reply.

'Don't ever let me hear you say that again, Jenny. That is ridiculous.' Martin sighed, shook his head and walked into the kitchen, but Jenny followed him, muttering as she changed the pronoun. 'He doth protest too much, methinks.'

'Anyway, why doesn't Vanessa go out with her sisters, the twins, now she's living down here? After all, they did grow up together.'

'She hasn't yet.' Jenny didn't elaborate on the reason. 'But she will do soon.'

'Well, she's been down here nearly a year already.'

'Vanessa told me that she's never been close to them,

151

because they're twins and they always have each other. She's always felt excluded. She's right about that because I can feel it myself when I'm with them.'

'I would have thought all four of you would meet up together now Vanessa's nearer.'

'That probably will happen, but at the moment it's easier to meet the twins as a pair, and I can show Vanessa around locally so she can get used to the area. After all, she is my sister.'

'Well, you've certainly done that.'

'Anyway, the twins aren't the slightest bit interested in the countryside. I always meet them in Horsham or we go together to their houses.'

But, even before Martin had spoken, Jenny had been thinking of how she could lessen her meetings with Vanessa.

Jenny stood in front of the sitting room window and watched as a teenage couple still wearing their school uniforms wandered hand in hand up the path towards the church. She was deciding how best to broach the subject.

'To be honest, Martin, I'm not that keen on going with her, but I can't let her down. Once I told her about our break and how relaxing it was, she was so looking forward to sharing the trip with her daughter. She said she needed a short holiday after the divorce and her move, and if we went together, she would be able to share a part of my childhood that she had missed. That's true, she's right about that, and having found her, it's hard for me to refuse to go with her.'

'I can see that. Let me check my diary. What week has she booked for?'

'Second week in May, after the May Day bank holiday and so no children around.' Jenny watched as Martin sauntered over to the oak desk in the corner of their sitting room, pulled open a drawer, removed his diary and flicked through the pages.

'Oh yes, I'd forgotten, I'm supposed to be seeing Daniel sometime in May. I've put a line through a couple of weekends that I'm free. They're only pencilled in at the moment, so perhaps I'll check with him and we might stay for a couple of nights somewhere. Father-and-son bonding trip.' He turned to grin at Jenny.

'You don't need to bond, you get on so well together.'

'Do I detect a hint of jealousy in that remark?'

Jenny sighed. 'Possibly.' She knew he was spot on, but not in the way he thought. She wasn't jealous of his relationship with his son. What she resented was that she didn't have the same relationship with Lorna. She was happy and certainly relieved that her daughter was finally enjoying her first job at the Art's Council after graduating, and also blatantly enjoying her new partner – they were all over each other like teenagers – whom she had met through work. He was a few years younger than Lorna and had three children of his own from his marriage and shared custody of them, so she seldom had any spare time to go out with Jenny. Their only contact was an occasional lightning visit on Lorna's way home from work, or more frequently a phone call to ask her to pick up Storm or Hector from some after-school activity. She often wondered why those children were never left to play on their own or be bored, which Jenny thought was essential for a child's imagination and development. It was no wonder they were so demanding, expecting her to amuse them all the time when she minded them. 'I'll phone and tell her that our trip's on then. It will be a cheap holiday for me, that's for sure. Vanessa even said that she would love to show us South Africa sometime, if we ever needed a winter break. You know, Natal around Pietermaritzburg and Durban – the area where she grew up – so I can share her memories too.'

'We'll certainly take her up on that then. Do you know, it might technically be spring here but I'm freezing, so I'm going to put the heating on before we eat. Why don't you have a think where we could go this Sunday. It's about time we had a full day out, somewhere different from around here. The forecast is for it to be warmer by then. We can stop for a pub meal and that can be our bonding experience.' Martin flashed a grin to Jenny as he climbed the stairs.

30

Despite her reservations, Jenny enjoyed showing Vanessa around Guernsey. They visited the same places she had shown Martin and shared her childhood memories. But as soon as Jenny had mentioned Lihou Island and its ancient causeway to Vanessa, she pestered Jenny to take her there. So, on the third day of their trip – after checking the island's website – they drove in their hire car around the north-west corner of the island to Lihou. Jenny had double-checked the times the causeway was open that day, so they waited in their car until eleven minutes past eleven. Once certain that the tide was on its way out, and that, as far as they could see, the causeway was clear of water, they took their beach towels, enough food for the day, and ventured onto the stony path. Some areas were still wet and slippery with seaweed from the outgoing tide. The crying of gulls made conversation impossible as they gingerly picked their way across to Lihou. They walked around the island looking at the areas cordoned off for the nesting seabirds. It was a sultry day for the middle of May and, finding a smooth-faced rock to lean against, they lay their towels down on a tiny, pebbly beach to sunbathe. After eating their lunch, they sauntered once more past the remains of the Priory of St Mary and then returned to their beach towels and lay down for some more sunbathing. After a short while, Jenny suddenly sat up, checked her watch and peered out at the sea and then turned to where Vanessa lay sprawled out on her stomach and fast asleep on her towel.

'Vanessa, wake up. Vanessa, we need to go back now, wake up.' She patted her shoulder.

'What is it? What's the matter?' Vanessa sighed and reluctantly turned over, raised her head and then supporting herself on her elbows, peered through her sunglasses. 'What are you worried about? The tide isn't coming in yet. Look, it's way out still. We can stay longer, surely? I'm really enjoying it here, it's so relaxing in the sun and our first warm day.'

'The website and the notice board said we must be back off the causeway twenty minutes before it closes at two-forty-five and it's two-thirty already. I know it looks as if the tide's a long way out, but sometimes that's deceiving. It can be out in one place and creeping in on another. They said the currents were dangerous here. You read that too.' Previous newspaper articles about holidaymakers in various places being cut off by in-coming tides surfaced in Jenny's memory. 'The website said to make sure to allow at least twenty minutes to cross. It took us longer than that to get over here.'

Vanessa dropped back onto the pebbles. 'I'm not ready to go back yet, Jenny. It took longer coming over because the tide had only just gone out and it was slippery. It's dry now, so it will be easier and quicker. We don't need twenty minutes to cross.'

'But it might not be easier. I can't see from here and we can't risk being cut off. The causeway's a quarter of a mile long. I'm not a local and the signs both said to allow at least twenty minutes, didn't they? We've been here for over three hours. We can't risk it, Vanessa.' Jenny stood up, shook the sand off her beach towel and, picking up her bag, began walking towards the causeway. She turned round. 'Are you coming?' she said as Vanessa flopped back down on her towel.

'It's much too early to go back, Jenny. I can't see what you are worried about? The tide is still way out. I like a bit of excitement, and we can always swim back if we have to. It's not far and it's not going to be deep.'

'But you don't know about the currents, Vanessa. It's not just about the depth,' Jenny shouted back at Vanessa and carried on walking to the start of the causeway.

*

The following day was wet, so they decided to spend the morning in their room at the same hotel in St Peter Port where Jenny had stayed the previous year. 'So, Martin was OK about you coming with me then?'

'Yes, he was. I was a bit worried about mentioning it, as we've been out together quite a lot since you moved down, and he'd been making noises about us not going out anywhere together lately, but he was fine about it. I didn't know, but he'd already arranged to go somewhere with his son this month; they usually do once a year.' Jenny decided this was the moment to bring up the subject of their frequent meetings into the conversation.

'I did wonder what he would say. I do realise that we've seen a lot of each other lately. You've been so good, Jenny, just like an older sister should be, making me feel welcome and showing me around, so different from the twins. Also, I've loved our lunches together at your house. Martin's a lovely man, I can see now why you couldn't tell him the truth.'

Jenny looked over at her sister.

'Don't look so startled. I wouldn't have told him either if I had been you.'

'As I said before, Vanessa, I hardly think about it now. It's been so many years.'

'Look, Jenny, I completely understand, but some people might not.'

'Might not what?'

'You know, understand. It is against the law, isn't it?'

'I'm going to make us some coffee.' Jenny folded her newspaper and slid down from her bed where she had been resting.

'Oh, Jenny. I'm so sorry, I didn't mean to upset you, I shouldn't have mentioned it, and I'm sorry about yesterday too. You know, moaning about leaving Lihou and spoiling our day. It was stupid of me; I did leave it too late, the tide was lapping around my feet and getting deeper when I ran after you. You were right, it could have been dangerous.'

'Yes, it could have been, that's why the notices are on the beach and on the website, but you didn't spoil our day,' Jenny lied, remembering how she had waited anxiously at the end of the causeway – watching the tide creep ever closer over the stone slabs – for Vanessa to join her. 'I just wasn't expecting you to say what you just said, that's all. It came as a shock. But it's OK, I'll make the coffee.' Jenny took the kettle from its stand on the hotel table and walked into the bathroom.

'Jenny, I want to say that I'm so pleased that you found me. You've changed my life. I wasn't in a good place before. It's very difficult leaving the country you were born and brought up in, and then the divorce. It's so hard to feel at home without those roots and childhood friends.'

'Yes, I'm pleased I found you too. I realise now that roots are very important, and I understand how difficult it must have been for all of you to leave South Africa. But your daughter's good to you though, isn't she?'

'Well, as you know, she's been down to visit me a couple of times. I thought she'd visit more often. You must come over and meet her. Well, I did invite you, didn't I, but you were working on that day. Unfortunately, she never gives me much notice. Hopefully, next time you'll be free.'

Jenny thought back to when Vanessa had invited her to meet her daughter; it had been on the day she usually worked. 'Yes, I really would like to meet her; after all, she is my niece. I've never had any nieces or nephews before I met you all.'

'You will meet her. I'll make sure of that.'

*

'I'm so sorry, Jackie, to have missed you the last time you came down here. Unfortunately, I couldn't make it that day,' Jenny said one month later as she walked into the tiny room and smiled at the young woman with long, straight, blonde hair who was sitting on the edge of the leather sofa. Vanessa followed her into the room and sat down on a chair under the window and beckoned Jenny to sit in the armchair opposite.

'I'm pleased to meet you too, Jenny. Mum's told me so much about you. How helpful you've been while she settles down here and everything. It's so lovely for her to live by the sea; she's always lived inland before. Thank goodness she likes her job at the sports ground. I'm into athletics myself, like mother like daughter, but I'm nowhere near as good at sport as she was.'

Jenny noticed how slim Jackie was, *even slimmer than her mother*, she thought with chagrin. 'You haven't got much of an accent. Not like your mother.'

'Don't forget, Jenny, I lived much longer in South Africa than Jackie has,' interrupted Vanessa.

'Yes, I spent a lot of time, once I qualified, working abroad. Mostly Singapore and San Francisco. Because my firm's international, we've offices in most developed countries.'

'Yes, she's done so well for herself and I'm very proud of her,' added Vanessa.

'Yes, accents are strange,' said Jenny, trying to avoid looking at the bright-orange flowers on what remained of the wallpaper that still dominated the tiny room. 'I know a Pakistani couple, and the husband has been working here for years and I still can't always understand him, especially when he talks quickly. Whereas his wife, who has never lived anywhere else until she came here two years ago, speaks perfect English with only a very slight trace of an accent. I once read somewhere that if a child learns a second language before the age of five, he will always speak that language without an accent. It's strange, isn't it? Anyway, it must have been amazing to work in such interesting cities.'

'Yes, it has been. I would never have been able to visit them otherwise. But it's not easy being away from home. I can still speak Afrikaans. We were all bilingual in South Africa. Some of the black people often spoke two or three local languages as well as English and Afrikaans.'

Vanessa passed Jenny a plate of chocolate biscuits. 'Come on, help me out, otherwise I'll put on weight, and I can't let that happen in my job. The trouble is, I can never say no to chocolate when it's in the house.'

'I'm the same about chocolate, but you're so slim, Vanessa, and Jackie's the same; neither of you have to worry about getting fat.'

'I'm sorry I haven't had time to scrape off all the horrendous wallpaper. I can see you looking at it.'

'It's difficult not to.' Jenny smiled.

'I can see the family likeness, Jenny, apart from the colour of your eyes. Mum's are brown while yours are grey-green. Mum said you look like my grandfather. Unfortunately, I don't remember him much at all, only a couple of flashes from the past, but I have seen photos of him.'

'Yes, that's true. I do look like him. I have a photo of him when he was in his late twenties and in the army, which is lovely. It's easier to see a likeness when you're both about the same age. Not so easy when you are older,' Jenny added.

'We get along really well too, don't we, Jenny? Much better than I ever did with the twins. By the way, have you seen them lately?'

'Not since March, but I will see them again soon.' Jenny reached into her bag. 'Look, I've brought my camera, Vanessa, let me take a photo of both of you. If you can squeeze next to Jackie on the sofa, that will make it easier.'

Jacqueline turned to look at her mother, who nodded, stood up and stepped across to the sofa to sit next to her daughter. Jenny took two photos to ensure one was acceptable. Then Jackie offered to take a photo of Jenny and Vanessa together. Jenny thought as she moved over to the sofa, that this will be the first photo that she will have of them together. Vanessa never bought a camera to their meetings apart from their trip to the Seven Sisters, whereas the twins were always taking photos of each other and asking strangers to take one of the three of them together and sending copies on to Jenny so she had them to keep. They chatted for a further half hour, mostly about Vanessa's job as a coach at Hastings Athletics Club, and Jenny's at the solicitors, before Jacqueline stood up saying she had to leave, as she had to catch the train back to Birmingham. Jenny noticed that she was taller than Vanessa, at least five foot nine inches. Her last glimpse of Jackie was – as they stood on the doorstep of the cottage – of her tossing her long hair over her shoulder as she waved to them from the end of the path, and then disappeared.

'I'm so pleased to have met her at last, Vanessa. She's tall like you,' Jenny said as they went back inside the house.

'Yes, she is, but I haven't got her fair hair. She gets that from Dale.'

'Is she working at the moment? She didn't say and I didn't like to ask.'

'She doesn't normally say much about her work. She wants to forget about it when she's away from the office. I do know though that she finds it stressful sometimes. The last time we spoke on the phone, she was even talking about changing careers and wondering what else she could do. I don't like to keep asking. She'll tell me when she's ready. I just hope she doesn't go back to Jo'burg. Anyway, more tea before you leave?' Without waiting for a reply, Vanessa picked up the teapot from the coffee table and walked out of the room. As she left, Jenny realised that Jackie hadn't hugged or kissed her mother goodbye.

31

The next time Jenny met the twins, she mentioned that she had met Vanessa's daughter.

'You did? So she is in England now then?' queried Maddy.

'She said she moved here to be near her parents, but I don't know how long she's been here. I only went over to meet her and for some tea and cake as she was down here visiting Vanessa. She was pleased to meet me, but she couldn't stay long. It's quite a journey from Birmingham to Bexhill and back in one day.'

'Surely she could have stayed overnight at Vanessa's? But, perhaps she had to work the next day. Mind you, I'd be surprised if she has a good relationship with Vanessa. She wouldn't have told you, but she was in foster care for many years. She did go back to her mother for a while, but it didn't work out. Not sure why, Vanessa never told us, but we do know she returned to live permanently with her foster parents. She did well at school though, which was good.'

'Why was she in foster care?'

'We're not sure why, are we, Cathy? Vanessa just said

she couldn't cope and that she was a difficult child. But they only had the one, and Dale was very good. He did so much around the house as well as looking after Jackie. Not like most South African men.'

Cathy nodded in agreement. 'Yep, they're proper MCPs. Male chauvinist pigs in translation. I know I shouldn't class all men the same, and Dale certainly wasn't one, but the majority were when we were growing up. Not so much now though, I'm pleased to say. They've certainly evolved. We think there must have been more to it than just not coping for Jackie to be taken away from her parents and then not going back to live with them. Vanessa will never tell us. She may tell you though. But whatever happened in the past, she's done very well for herself. Last we heard from her, she had a good position in an accountant's office – some worldwide company in Jo'burg. She must have asked for a transfer – they have offices everywhere – with Dale and Vanessa being here now. It's not easy to move to England. If Gerrit hadn't been Dutch and from the EU, we would have had difficulty.'

'I've got a photo of her to show you.' Jenny reached into her raffia bag and pulled out the printed photo that she had taken of Jacqueline and Vanessa on the sofa. She passed it to Cathy.

'She looks older now, don't you think, Maddy?' Cathy screwed up her eyes as she examined the photo forensically with her twin. 'Of course, it was several years ago when we last saw her. Her hair seems lighter too and longer. They look a bit stiff sitting together like that.'

'She must have had that mole removed from her forehead; it was just above her eyebrow – sorry, beauty spot, that's what Vanessa always insisted on calling it,' Maddy added, looking at Jenny.

'She probably had it removed as a precaution, Maddy. You have to be careful of skin cancer in the southern hemisphere. Do you remember what happened to that girl in our class at school, Charlene Swart? She ignored a mole that had changed colour and was dead within a year. Vanessa looks very glamorous – shame about the tracksuit – but then she always did. She doesn't look any older; they could be sisters. Jackie's tall, of course, too, like her mother, and thin. But I don't remember her being as thin as that, and that's in a photo, too; they always manage to make you look fatter than you really are, as least they do me, unfortunately.' Cathy handed the photo back to Jenny. 'Thanks for showing us, but we've seen enough.'

'Look, let's arrange a family lunch at ours,' said Maddy. 'Say, two weeks from Sunday. It's been a while since you and Martin have been up. It's summer, so we can have a braai. The men are always keen to cook outdoors.'

32

Late-flowering cow parsley still edged both sides of the lane with white lace as Jenny drove slowly into the layby to avoid the pot holes and switched off the engine. She had been to visit Nicky in his new supported accommodation and saying goodbye always left her depressed. She could have driven straight back home, but she needed a detour across the Downs to lift her mood. She stared down into the Adur Valley and the red roofs of Steyning until her thoughts about Nicky and his life evaporated. Her gaze settled on a nearby hawthorn tree so heavy with blossom that it resembled the aftermath of a snowstorm as she thought back to her conversation with Vanessa the day before.

'I'm going to have to postpone our meetup tomorrow, Vanessa, I'm so sorry.' There was no response, so Jenny continued, 'It's Nicky, I'm going to have to go over to see him at his accommodation; he hasn't been well again. It's the move, I'm sure. Any change of routine is bad for him.'

'Can't Lorna go, or Rob? He is his father. We've planned this trip for ages.'

'I know, I was looking forward to it too. But Rob still works full-time so I need to go myself. I'm sorry it's such short notice.' Jenny was taken aback at Vanessa's words. If someone had said the same to her, she would have been disappointed, but she would have understood. 'Look, let's make another date, so we can look forward to that.'

'But it's been ages since we've been out together. Not since we came back from Guernsey. You couldn't make the last time I suggested meeting up.'

'I know, I feel bad about having to cancel tomorrow too.'

'Well don't go then, Jenn. He's an adult, he'll be OK, you can go and see him another day. You deserve a day out.'

For a moment, Jenny was tempted to agree. Perhaps she could see Nicky another day, but she was working the three days following. 'No, I'm sorry, Vanessa, I would never forgive myself if I didn't go and something happened to him. Can't we meet Tuesday next week instead?' Jenny knew she had a doctor's appointment that day, but she would cancel it.

'No, I can't get that day off work. That's a selection day for a couple of hopefuls for next year's Commonwealth Games.'

'Well, the following Tuesday then.'

'I'll have to let you know. It would be so much easier if you could see Nicky another day.'

'I know, but he's been quite unwell lately.'

'Jenn, your dinner's getting cold,' Martin shouted from the kitchen.

'Look, I've got to go, Vanessa, I'll call you tomorrow.' Jenny stood holding the receiver as the phone cut off.

A skylark fluttered down onto the field next to the layby as Jenny wondered if she should phone Vanessa that evening. She thought she ought to, being the one who cancelled their planned day out. It was understandable that Vanessa was upset, as she had also postponed their earlier arrangement. Yes, she decided, she would phone her, but then was worried how Vanessa would react. She had slammed the phone down on her, something she had never experienced before with anyone. *Perhaps*, she wondered, *this is how sisters behave with each other.* If she had arranged to meet her friend Gail and had to cancel, it would have been uncomplicated. Gail would have said it was a shame and at her suggestion of rearranging, they would immediately set up another day and that would be the end of the matter. She wouldn't be sitting her car worrying about phoning her. But then, they were old friends, not sisters. It was different with the twins, as apart from meeting them together for lunch or a tea, they also socialised together with their families, not as two individuals. She remembered girls at school complaining about their sisters, younger and older, saying what a pain they were. So that's obviously how it is with sisters, she decided. Jenny remembered her words to Martin when she had first found them, *I don't know how to be a sister.* She turned the ignition and drove down into the valley and home.

Jenny was pondering what to say to Vanessa while she stirred the korma sauce when the phone rang. 'I'll answer that, Martin, can you come in here and stir this?'

'Look, I'm sorry I put the phone down on you yesterday, Jenn, I felt so bad afterwards, that's why I'm calling you. Of course you had to go and see Nicky. It was selfish of me to complain.'

'That's OK, Vanessa,' Jenny said, relieved as she stared through the window at her neighbour walking Barker up the church path.

'No, it isn't. I shouldn't have done that. It's just that I was really looking forward to seeing you and finally visiting Ashdown Forest. I've never had a sister like you before.'

'Well, neither have I.'

'A sister is different to a friend, isn't she?'

'Yes, I'm discovering that too.'

'Look, let's do Tuesday next week as you said. I'm sure I can get one of the other coaches to stand in for me.'

'Yes, that's fine,' Jenny agreed, thinking she would phone the surgery tomorrow morning to cancel her appointment.

33

'When are you going to finish at the computer, Martin?' Jenny asked and sighed as she entered the attic room. 'What are you doing anyway?'

'I'm plotting the number of Purple Hairstreak butterflies at Ebenoe Common. Late summer is the best time for them. They seem to be increasing, which is good.'

Jenny laughed. 'That name always makes me smile. It's more like the words my hairdresser might say to me than the name of a butterfly.'

Martin swivelled round and smiled as he faced Jenny. 'What's up? You don't normally come up here when I'm working. You look worried.'

'I am worried. I need to talk to you about something.'

'Well, fire away then. I can come back to this.'

'It's about Vanessa.'

'What about her?'

'I feel ridiculous saying this, but I feel I have to keep making excuses so as not to meet up with her so often.'

'Why should you do that?'

'She wants to see me more than I want to see her. No,

that's wrong. It's not that I don't want to see her, just that I don't want to see her as often as she wants to see me.'

'That's not a problem, surely? Just tell her you can't meet up as often, she'll understand.'

'As I said, I keep making excuses and I can't carry on doing that.'

'I know you'll think this sounds sexist, but a man wouldn't have this problem, he'd just say, "Sorry, mate, but I can't see you for a while, women, you know? I'll give you a ring when I'm free." His friend would then nod knowingly, and that would be the end of the matter. It wouldn't be a problem.'

'Well, you're right about one thing. That is the most sexist remark I've ever heard you say.'

'But it's true and it's the only answer, isn't it? Why keep making excuses when you could just tell her the reason?'

'I know it sounds ridiculous. I suppose I feel bad that I have more going on in my life than she does, and now that she's been living down here for a year, I can't give her as much time as I have been doing.'

'But that's not your fault, is it? That you have more going on. It happens to everyone at different times. You've never had a problem telling Gail you can't see her, have you? And Vanessa's your sister.'

Jenny thought, *this is so like Martin, logical as ever.* 'That's just it, she's my sister, not my friend, so I feel I have to see her. I thought she might have made some friends down here now; she has, but not to go out with. Her daughter lives in Birmingham, and she told me that she's always felt left out by the twins.'

'But that's nothing to do with you, Jenn. Next time she asks to meet up, ask her over here for dinner instead. She won't feel left out then, will she? And you won't have to meet up with her. I'd like to see her again anyway, so we all win, and you two can relax together while I cook.' Martin swivelled around in his chair and squinted at the graph on the computer screen before resuming tapping in the data from his notebook. 'Have you ever seen a Purple Hairstreak, Jenn?'

'No, I haven't.' Jenny stood staring at the screen for a full minute before turning around and going downstairs.

*

'Thanks for asking me over for dinner. It's never good having to eat on your own all the time and Friday always seems worse somehow than other days. It's lovely to see you again, Martin, it's been too long. You look well, so Jenny must be doing something right. No need to go into the details.' She smiled at him.

'I'm in the middle of a survey of Purple Hairstreak butterflies at the moment. Late summer is the best time of year for them, so I'm not around a lot just now. But I'm always here Mondays and Fridays though. Start, Vanessa, don't wait for us,' said Martin as he placed a plate of spaghetti bolognaise in front of her.

'So, you're a good cook, Martin, as well as good-looking. You don't mind me flirting with your husband, do you, Jenn? Not many opportunities at the sports stadium and I must keep in practice.'

Jenny noticed that Vanessa had abandoned her

tracksuit for a pair of tight-fitting jeans and a bright-yellow top. 'I would have thought that would be the ideal place, all those muscular athletes, driven by testosterone.'

'One-track minds, excuse the pun, I've had a few come on to me. Once they knew I was divorced, they left me in no doubt as to what was on offer. But I don't want a one-night stand. Well, I suppose I might, depends on what they look like.' She smiled.

'Well, I have a job to prize Martin away from his computer lately with his involvement in his survey.'

'I could think of something to prize him away.' Vanessa smiled at her sister. 'Don't look so worried, Jenny – joke.'

'Jenn's been a bit low lately, haven't you?'

'Oh, why didn't you tell me? We could have met up.'

'It's OK, Vanessa, the meal was Martin's idea, cook us both a meal and meet up at the same time.'

'That's so sweet of you, Martin. The bolognese sauce is excellent, much better than the jars that I resort to. Anyway, I've got an announcement to make and I think you're both going to be impressed. I've registered and been accepted for an Open University degree course and I start in October. It's environmental studies, a BSc course. I can hardly believe it myself. I'm so excited about it. I'm planning on fitting it around my coaching work and it will help me to meet new people. I realised in the summer that I've been leaning on you a bit too much, Jenny. It's been over a year now since I moved down here. You've got your family locally, so you have more going on than I do, so naturally you can't always meet up. Also, I don't want to spoil our relationship by being too needy.'

'You're not needy, Vanessa,' said Jenny.

'Well, anyway, that's what I've done. I didn't tell you before because I wanted to make sure I'd been accepted onto the course. I could have done an access course first because I haven't done any studying for a long time – years, in fact – but I decided to jump straight in because I wanted to get started with the subject matter, so hopefully it will be OK.'

Martin looked up from his spaghetti. 'I'm very impressed, Vanessa. It's a very good idea and I'm sure you'll be fine. It's a big commitment though. I did the same thing myself years ago when the Open University first started in the 1970s. Finally, after six years, I received my BSc. It took up nearly all of my spare time though, and I was working full-time at the bank in Southampton then. Marilyn, my ex-wife, used to moan about it, as Daniel was only young then. But it was worth it. I've never regretted it. It enabled me to have the job I'd always wanted. I could give you a few tips, not that you'll need them.'

'I can't carry on coaching full-time for ever, I'm beginning to find it harder to keep up with the youngsters. I'm fifty now, so I need to have another option. This way, I could perhaps do some voluntary conservation work, which would help with any future job application. That's what Jenny told me you do for the Trust, isn't it?'

*

Martin laughed out loud as he helped Jenny wipe the chocolate from the profiteroles off the dessert plates. 'Well, there you are, problem solved. Vanessa even came up with

175

the solution herself. She's realised she's been taking up too much of your time.'

'But, why has she chosen environmental studies?'

'Why not? She's interested in the subject. What else would she choose – ancient history? No good studying a subject you're not interested in. My God, Jenny, are you never satisfied?'

34

'It's so good to see you both again,' Jenny said, giving each twin a hug. 'I'm sorry it's been so long. Family and work seem to have taken over my life lately. I won't leave it so long next time.'

'We were wondering what had happened to you, weren't we, Maddy? Let's sit here away from those screaming children. I thought, not meeting in the school holidays, we'd be spared that noise.'

'So, have you seen more of Vanessa lately? Is that why we've been neglected?' Maddy asked, smiling at Jenny as they as they settled back into the café armchairs.

'Time for me to get our drinks. Same as usual, Jenny?' asked Cathy, pushing her chair back. 'If those two children keep on screaming, I'm not going to be responsible for what I say to their mother.'

'Sorry, I shouldn't have mentioned her, but it's been a while since we've met and Cathy will ask me later what we spoke about. She likes playing the wronged wife, but she's not so squeaky clean herself.'

'You're right, I have been seeing quite a lot of Vanessa, that's one of the reasons why I haven't been able to meet up with you both. But I have some news about her. She's started an Open University degree course on environmental studies.'

'A degree course, are you sure?' asked Maddy.

'Yes, that's what she said.'

'Well, I certainly wasn't expecting that. As far as I remember, she was never academic; she didn't like studying, she was good at maths though. But she couldn't sit still for five minutes, always on the go. Sport was always her passion, and as we've said before, she was very good at it too. I think she did a diploma in sports management or sports science. I can't remember what exactly. Because we were so much older, Cathy and I were both married with young families when she was a teenager, so we didn't take much notice of what she was doing or see her that often.'

'There was something I wanted to ask you. Can you remember approximately how old her daughter was when she was taken into care? I can't ask Vanessa as she's never mentioned it to me, and I would never ask her anything about it, but it will help me to understand her a bit more.'

'You met her daughter, didn't you? I remember you showed us the photos. I think Jackie was about seven years old, so probably it would be the late 1980s. Vanessa was pregnant when they married. She was young, they both were, twenty-one I think, so yes, probably 1987, 1988. I'm pleased that you're in contact with her. I've always felt bad that I haven't kept in touch. But Cathy's never forgiven her. But as I said, once you've left, she'll soon want to know what we've been talking about.' Maddy smiled.

'Was it Johannesburg where she lived after they married?'

'Yes, Hillbrow, they were married there. I do remember their wedding. We were both there.'

*

Jenny sat in her car and stared at the small boy throwing bread for the Canada geese that had gathered expectantly on the small beach left by the shrinking waters of Falmer Pond. When Martin and herself had made the decision to live together, they had rented a small, flint cottage that stood next to the post office on the lane that ran along the south side of the pond. It was more the size of a lake than a pond, and she would always walk Toby around it twice a day, and if she had time, over the footbridge to the other half of Falmer Village that had been divided in two by the widening of the A27. It was while they were living there that she found out the identity of her birth mother. Thinking of that time distracted her from going over in her mind what she had just discovered about Vanessa. For the past two weeks, on the days she didn't work, she had been visiting the library at Sussex University, which she remembered had a large collection of South African newspapers. The university campus lay on the northern side of the A27 and was one of the first universities built after the war, opening its doors to students in 1962. It had fostered close links with South Africa during the apartheid years, with many ANC members studying there, including Thambo Mbeki, who replaced Nelson Mandela as president. Working and raising her children had fractured Jenny's memories of those years, leaving only a few scenes in her mind of rioting and subsequent killings in the townships that she had glimpsed on the evening news. She had been surprised to hear from the twins that her birth father had once been a member of the ANC. But replacing her deficient knowledge of that time was not the reason she had just been pouring over microfilm of the *Johannesburg Star* newspaper for the years 1987 and 1988, although she had inadvertently increased her knowledge of what had happened in those years from the headlines.

She had reached January 1988 when she saw a headline on page three. *Hillbrow Athletic Star Jailed for Five Years for Attempted Murder.* Vanessa Pienaar was described as a sport's coach, with a successful career in athletics, who had represented Natal in numerous competitions. She had been found guilty of attacking her husband Dale with a kitchen knife in a jealous rage. His injuries being severe enough for him to be given an emergency operation and hospitalised for two weeks. Mitigating circumstances were stated by the psychiatrist called by her defence counsel, as being her recently diagnosed mental health condition of manic depression, which the judge hoped she would receive the appropriate treatment for in prison. She had pleaded guilty, and as she had no previous convictions, the judge passed the minimum sentence of five years. Her husband was standing by her. He had initially been reluctant to press charges, but had changed his mind after being told that his wife would receive the help she needed in prison. *So*, Jenny thought, *that must have been when Jackie had been taken into care.* Jenny wondered if she had witnessed the attack. Vanessa would never tell her about this, and why should she? She could have been severely provoked. It sounded from the article as if Dale had been having an affair or Vanessa had thought he was. She may have been suffering from premenstrual tension, aggravated by her mental illness. Who knows what anyone can be capable of if provoked? She wouldn't tell Martin what she had read, and she certainly wouldn't tell the twins; she was sure they, or especially Cathy, would have told her by now if they had known the full story.

35

'I wasn't expecting my birth mother to have passed away, Jenny, she was only in her forties,' Briony told Jenny over the phone.

'Well, no, I'm so sorry to hear that, Briony. She was still young. But how did you find out?'

'I contacted Australia House and they were really helpful, telling me who to contact in Melbourne. Apparently she married Jurgen, the playwright she'd left England with in the 1950s. So, I had her married name and where they were living. I wrote to her husband, who told me the sad news. But the best thing is they had a child, a girl, so I do have a half-sister after all. Jurgen's lovely; he's told me all about them both and sent me photos of my mother and their daughter. He even said I could stay with them if I wanted to visit Melbourne at any time.'

'I'm so thrilled for you, Briony. So do you think you will visit them?'

'Yes definitely, and I'm so pleased that I didn't give up searching, so that's why I'm phoning, to tell you and to say thank you.'

With only occasional telephone contact with Vanessa since she had announced her decision to start her university course, Jenny relaxed. She phoned Vanessa regularly, usually at the weekend, to find out how she was managing. Each time Vanessa would reply, 'Great, I'm really enjoying the challenge. I've learnt so much already. Busy, of course, trying to fit everything in, work, chores, you know what it's like.'

Jenny did know, and would say, 'I'll let Martin know, he'll be really pleased.'

'Oh yes, please tell him. We must meet up again soon.'

'Yes, we will,' Jenny said, but weeks passed without Vanessa arranging a date to meet.

*

The weather was perfect for their autumn break to Vienna. Arriving tourists trailing small, multicoloured cases wandered past their outside table at the Café Diglas, which lay around the corner from St Stephen's Dom and the waiting fiacres. Deciding to ignore the trams that trundled down Wiedner Hauptstrasse, they had walked from their hotel towards Ressel Park. Taking a shortcut through the streets towards Karlskirche, Jenny stopped when she spotted six brass plaques embedded into the pavement. She recognised the plaques as the same type she had seen from their earlier trip to Berlin. Strauss, Grabkowicz and Goldstein, the names of Viennese families, were inscribed on the plaques and the dates they were forcibly removed from their homes in 1942. Jenny thought of Gordon, her birth father. By that date, he was imprisoned in Silesia, not that far from where they now stood, but he had survived the war to live his life, unlike these unfortunate souls of whom only their names, dates of their deportations and deaths remained. A lasting memorial that they had lived, loved and worked in the city.

'You know, I think I'll have to press Vanessa for a meetup date when we get home. It seems strange not seeing her for such a long time. I actually miss seeing her, now I'm not meeting her so often.'

'She must be busy with her course, so that's good. Ask her over for a meal, that will give her a break, and you can tell her about our trip,' said Martin.

'No, I think I'd prefer to meet her on my own somewhere. I can't believe it's taken us so long to come here; I've always wanted to visit Vienna. So many beautiful buildings and another capital city off my list.'

'No, not one city, two off your list. What about our boat trip on the Danube? You're forgetting Bratislava. It may have only been an afternoon, but at least we visited it and walked around the old town.'

'True, how could I forget it, especially that poppy-seed cake? Well, I think my feet have recovered now from all this walking. Let's order, I know what you're having, and that will be your third in three days.'

'Yes, and you'll be right.' Martin squeezed Jenny's hand. 'Apfelstrudel for you too then?'

36

Lesser Hawkbit – *Leontodon saxatilis*, Autumn Lady's Tresses – *Spiranthes spiralis*. Jenny loved saying the Latin name out loud, picturing long, flowing, blonde locks as she wrote it in her notebook. Scabious – *Knautia arvensis* and Centuary – *Centaurium*… Jenny wrote their common names whilst trying to remember and write their Latin names, but Centuary's escaped her. For the last two years, she had been making several visits to local churchyards to record the wild flowers that grew in the grassland around the graves. She decided that this would be her final survey. She had previously completed Patcham and Newtimber churchyards, and as it was now October, this would be her last visit to Pyecombe. Reducing her working days to two each week and not seeing so much of Vanessa had freed up time for her to start and complete a third churchyard as part of the National Survey. The churchyards had been richer botanically than she had imagined. Both Patcham and Pyecombe's were on downland, so pyramid and bee orchids had been recorded as well as the usual chalk grassland species. Newtimber Church lay down a lane under the northern escarpment of the Downs, so had clumps of primroses, wood anemones and bluebells. Jenny walked over to the wooden bench where she had left her backpack and, undoing the zip, placed her notebook and pen away for the final time. A few late-fledging house martins flew over her, but the swifts that had nested in the church tower and had scythed through the sky above her screaming had already left.

Fifteen minutes later, as she closed the front door behind her, she heard Martin say, 'Don't worry, I'll get Jenny to call you when she comes back, see you soon.'

'Who's that?'

'Vanessa.'

'Oh, I only spoke to her on Sunday.'

'I know, she's really apologetic, but she sounded in a bit of a state. Do you think you could call her back? I'm sure she's fine. I was just about to put some baked potatoes in the oven, so I'll carry on.'

'Well, believe it or not, I've just completed the final survey, that's three churchyards done and dusted,' Jenny said, flinging her backpack onto the sofa. 'I'll call her back now as I might not feel like it once we've eaten.'

Her call was answered immediately. 'Oh, Jenny, thanks for phoning back so soon. I didn't want to say anything to Martin, and I kept putting off calling you or saying anything when we spoke on Sunday because I didn't want to admit it.'

'Admit what?'

'That I'm going to find the course really difficult. It looked fine at first when I looked through the textbooks. I thought yes, I can do this, but these last weeks – I'm not so sure.'

'Not sure about what?'

'The course. I'll be OK on biology, as I did quite a lot of that for my sports diploma. But it's the maths and chemistry that I know I won't be able to do.'

'Have you mentioned this to your tutor?'

'Yes, and he's been really good. But I still can't get my head around the formulae and symbols. I'm hoping I'm just panicking about what I've taken on.'

'I'm sorry to hear that, but I'm sure it's not going to be as bad as what you think. Why don't you come over here and bring your books, I'm sure Martin will be able to reassure you.'

'Oh, Jenny, you're the best sister ever. Shall I come this Friday, in the afternoon? I remember Martin's usually around then.'

'But I'm not. I always work on Fridays.'

'That doesn't matter. I'll be there when you get back and I'll buy some fish and chips so that you and Martin don't have to bother to prepare a meal for me. That will help you too, and we can chat after dinner. It's been a long time since we've seen each other.'

'Yes, it has,' Jenny agreed. 'I'll just check with Martin first and then I'll call you back.'

'I feel such an idiot, Jenny. I thought I would be able to cope, but I was never particularly academic, but I was good at maths. Can you tell Martin it's just a blip? Don't tell him I'm worried. As you say, I'm sure I'll be fine, I've probably been overthinking things.'

'OK, I'll call you back later after we've eaten.' Jenny replaced the receiver and stood staring out of the window as an elderly woman walking a bulldog struggled up the hill. But her thoughts were about Vanessa.

37

The unmistakable aroma of fish and chips assaulted Jenny as she opened the front door. Hanging her coat in the understairs cupboard next to Vanessa's, a familiar perfume unsettled her. She stood staring at the coat, unwilling to go into the kitchen, but listening to their conversation.

'I don't know why they always overdo the amount of chips. I should have bought two bags instead of three.' There was a rustling of paper from the kitchen.

'Don't worry about that, Vanessa. I'm not complaining.' Martin's voice was heard over the clatter of plates. 'Thanks for going to get them. Jenny should be back soon. Oh, talk of the devil, there you are, bang on time. Sit yourself down. Look what Vanessa's bought for us.'

'Yes, I made sure I caught the earlier bus. Thank you for treating us, Vanessa. I always buy too many chips too.'

'Are you OK, Jenny? You look a bit, I don't know, worried.'

'No, I'm fine. It's good to see you. It's been quite a while. You've had your hair cut. It suits you shorter,' said Jenny, thinking how it made her look younger, as did her jeans and V-neck jumper. *No tracksuit today*, she thought.

'Well, I'm certainly making up for not seeing you both for so long, I've been here since just after two and Martin's been brilliant taking me through the textbook and making sure I understand each chapter.' She beamed at Martin. 'I feel much more confident already. I think, like I said on the phone, I was just panicking.'

'I'm sure you'll be able to cope, Vanessa, once you get used to the terminology. It's scary when you start a subject that you've no previous experience of. I was the same about equations when I started my science degree. I wasn't that good with maths at school, but my tutor explained them so well, it made such a difference. When the OU first opened its doors – so to speak – we had more tutorials than it appears they give you now.'

'Yes, they have cut the tutorials down, someone else said that. I loved biology at school, and what maths I needed for my sports diploma wasn't nearly so hard as some look in this textbook. Also, I thought I was good at maths, so perhaps it's because I'm older now?'

'I think it's more likely to be because you've been out of the habit of studying for a long time, so you're bound to find it a struggle at first. Well, I'm glad I've helped by showing you how I do them. Don't throw that sheet away with my writing on though.'

'As if I would, you're my knight in shining armour. You're lucky to have him, Jenny.'

'Don't praise him too much, he's lucky to have me.'

'I can't argue with that.' Martin smiled at Vanessa.

'You'd better not. If you've both finished eating, I'll make us some coffee.' Jenny pushed her chair back, and lifting the kettle off its stand, filled it with water.

'You haven't eaten all your fish and chips, Jenn. Sit down, there's no rush for coffee.'

'It's a long way for Vanessa to drive back, it's dark and I think it's started raining.' Jenny rummaged in the cupboard for another mug as the kettle began to boil.

'Martin, would you mind if I came over again if I'm still having problems? I promise I won't make a habit of it. Sorry, Jenny, of course, I hope it's OK with you too?'

Before Jenny could reply, Martin said, 'Just give us a call, so long as you bring fish and chips.'

'But, remember, only two bags of chips next time, Vanessa, I hate wasting food,' said Jenny.

'It won't be wasted, Jenn, it can always go out for the fox,' said Martin. 'Do you have foxes where you are?'

'My neighbour two doors down puts food out for them. Some nights I've heard them screaming, it's such a horrible noise. When I first heard it, I thought some poor person was being murdered.'

'Yes, it's spooky, they call mostly in the mating season.'

Vanessa gulped down the last of her coffee. 'Thank you for that, Jenny. Well, I suppose I'd better be off. As you say, it's quite a drive.' Vanessa stood up from the table with Martin joining her.

'I'll go and fetch your coat for you. Don't forget your books and papers.'

'Let me thank you properly.'

Jenny watched as Vanessa stepped forward to give Martin a hug followed by a kiss on his cheek. She then followed him out of the kitchen.

'Well, she certainly appreciated my help,' said Martin as he sat back down at the kitchen table.

'Didn't she just. If she needed it in the first place.'

'Why do you say that?'

'No reason, just that I remember Maddy saying that she was always good at maths, not like them, or me, come to that.'

'Well, she's probably forgotten what she was taught. It's been a long time since she was at school or college. You seemed in a rush to get rid of her. Or am I reading it wrong? It's not that bad outside. It isn't raining.'

'You're reading it wrong, Martin. I'm tired, that's all. I just want to relax on my own before an early night. I'll give her a call next week to arrange a meetup. Just the two of us. It's been quite a while.'

38

2010

'What's this in aid of?' Martin said as he spotted the full wine glasses and a bottle of Prosecco laid out on the kitchen table.

'I've just been accepted as a volunteer advisor at Citizens Advice. They called earlier to let me know.'

'Oh, God, sorry, I'd forgotten you went for that interview. Are you sure you won't find it too much? All those people with problems. You already deal with bereaved people as it is.'

'But I only do two days a week at the office now, and this will be just one day a week and it's not dealing with bereaved people, the problems are much more varied; benefits, for example. So, I don't think so. As a volunteer, I can please myself whether I work or not on some days. With my research experience and the years spent with clients at work, I know I'd be good at it, and they seem to think so too. It's good to give something back. Don't forget, I don't see Vanessa so much now she's busy with her course, and with the grandchildren being older, Lorna doesn't need me so much as she did on my days off, so I have plenty more time on my hands.'

'More time to devote to me then.' Martin grinned, pulling her towards him and wrapping his arms around her. He kissed her long on her lips. 'Can you feel something hard?' he whispered in her ear.

Jenny felt herself blushing, thinking for a moment that they were too old now to behave like teenagers. But, flushed with her good news and not helped by Martin staring into her eyes while rubbing her hand against his trousers, any objection quickly slipped away. *We are only in our early sixties*, she rationalised, *plenty of couples marry again at our age.*

He sighed. 'Why don't we go upstairs and celebrate properly? I'll bring the glasses if you bring the bottle.'

Ten minutes later, they lay on top of the bed with Jenny thinking that their lovemaking had an urgency about it that hadn't happened for a long time. Sex had become so infrequent that Jenny often wondered whether it was still worthwhile replenishing her oestrogen pessaries. She assumed this was just something that happened at their ages, but neither of them had the courage to bring the subject up. She was surprised how quickly she had climaxed, although not with the same intensity as when she was younger. As soon as she had lain back on the duvet, Martin had undone her jeans, pulling them down over her hips as he unbuttoned and unzipped his trousers. Then, stretching her panties to one side, he entered her – not bothering to remove his trousers as he usually did, as if frightened that she might change her mind. A few deep thrusts, then with a moan he cried out. Jenny, pushing herself against him, followed seconds later. Martin sighed and lay on top of her, exhausted, until he slipped out of her, their wetness seeping out with him.

'Oh, fuck, that quickie felt so good,' he whispered, 'excuse my language, Jenn, but very appropriate, don't you think? We should do this more often. Why don't we, for God's sake? We're not old. You enjoyed it too.'

'Yes, of course I did. So you don't think we're too old, do you?' Jenny shivered as she said the words, imagining Lorna's reaction if she could see them now. Quickly discarding the thought, she reached across to the bedside table for the box of tissues that in the past few years had more prosaic uses than pleasurable ones.

'Not by your reaction, we're not. We're both healthy; don't ask me to do it again though. You know, I often wonder whether you regret us not having our own child. Of course, it's too late now.'

'No, I don't, I really don't, Martin. You must believe that. We're happy as we are, just the two of us.'

'That's good, I'd hate to think that perhaps I should have done more to persuade you. So, when do you start this volunteering?'

'Wednesday next week. There's three months of training, though, before I can talk to or see clients face to face.'

'Well, so long as you don't overstretch yourself. We need to make time for more of this.' He leaned over and kissed her, his hand stroking her between her legs. He whispered, 'You could come again though, even if I can't. You always used to, and more than twice sometimes.'

'Just carry on doing that then,' Jenny muttered

breathlessly until, with a moan, she cried out for the second time.

'There you are, I knew you could.'

Jenny reached down and, as she playfully fingered his wet penis asked, 'Do you fancy Vanessa?'

'Well, she's very attractive, like you.' He grinned at her.

'You do then, I know she likes you and thinks you're good-looking.'

'Well, she would, wouldn't she? I've helped her, and I'm not bad for my age, am I? A bit grey around the temples now though, but that doesn't matter. I haven't put on much weight and the important bit still works, I've just proved that, and you still fancy me.' He grinned. 'But she's your sister, for God's sake. Surely you don't think I'd ever make a pass at her, Jenn?'

'No, I don't think that, but she might come on to you.' In their shared intimacy, Jenny found it easier to express her worry.

'Don't be ridiculous. In the unlikely event that she did, I wouldn't respond, would I?'

'You might not be able to help yourself, even if you regretted it afterwards.'

'This is a crazy conversation, Jenny. I'm not some horny teenage boy, but if you carry on doing what you're doing, I might be able to act like one after all.'

'I'll stop then. Too much for one day,' she said, wiping her hand with a tissue. 'Let's finish our drinks, then we'd better change this duvet cover.'

39

'You can't just give up, Vanessa. You've only been studying for a few months and you only said last week you were doing OK.'

'But, I wasn't, Jenny. I don't know why I said that on the phone. I suppose I didn't want to admit it to myself, especially after Martin encouraged me so much. But coming out today has made me realise, see things clearer, and stop kidding myself. I feel so much better finally admitting it. I thought I could do it, but I can't, and I won't be able to.'

The two women wandered side by side as they walked along the Ouse Valley Path. Jenny had suggested to Vanessa the day before that if she were free, she could join her after her session at Citizens Advice. They had parked and met in a lane at Southease where a wooden bridge carries the South Downs Way across the river. The sun was low in the sky and reed buntings chattered and fluttered in the rushes that bordered the path as they walked northwards.

'Why don't you come over and speak to Martin again?'

'No, it's no good. He will think I'm an idiot if I come over again. Suppose I still can't cope. I can't keep coming over for help. No, my mind's made up. It's stressing me out too much and I can't keep talking about it anymore either. Are you sure it's not too far to walk to Rodmell and back?'

'No, it's not that far. We can have a bite to eat and a drink there. No need for us to bother to cook later then.'

'I don't know what I'd do without you, Jenny.'

'You've still got your coaching job, and if you're really sure about giving up on the OU course, you could look around for something else to study that's not so demanding, perhaps a certificate or diploma course, or you could even change your job. There's no rush, take your time to think about it.'

'Yes, you're right. I jumped into this degree course without giving it enough thought. It would have been better if I had done the access course. I was advised to. I tend to do that, jump straight in and then everything goes belly up.'

'Next time, run any ideas across me first. That may help.'

'I had my heart set on that course – something to study that I really enjoy.'

'You could tell Jackie what you've decided and hopefully she'll come down and support you. Or, if she's busy, why not go up and visit her?'

'She's not up there anymore, Jenny.'

'Oh, you didn't tell me that. Where is she?' A mewing sound made Jenny stop walking and look up. 'Look, a buzzard, Vanessa, flying towards those trees. Have a look through the binoculars. You wouldn't know, but only a few years ago, we never saw buzzards in the south east or anywhere in England. Wales was the nearest place to see them. Now they're almost common here and it was the same with kites. I actually spotted one over Ditchling last week, they were only ever seen in mid Wales and they were down to only a few pairs.'

'She's gone back to Jo'burg. We had a big row. Things have never been easy between us. I wasn't the best mother when she was young.'

'Well, who is? It's the hardest job in the world, Vanessa, and I can't say I was perfect either, as Lorna never stops reminding me.'

'It was a bit more than the usual mother-and-daughter troubles. We never really bonded, and I was ill quite a lot when she was a small child.'

Jenny remembered the newspaper article she had read at the university. 'I'm sorry to hear that.'

'Look, I'll carry the binoculars now, they're quite heavy. Is that Rodmell over there?' Vanessa pointed across to the north west, where a church spire rose above the cottage roofs.

'Yes, that's it. I'm so sorry to hear she's gone back. When did that happen?'

'Oh, last year, that was when I decided to apply for the degree course. To help take my mind off it.'

Jenny remembered the afternoon last May in Vanessa's house when she was introduced to her daughter. It must have been soon after that. A signpost pointed to a path branching off to the left, which they took and approached a field with a newly painted cricket pavilion. 'We're nearly there, the pub's up the lane on the left, on the Lewes Road. Monk's House is down the lane to the right. It's now owned by the National Trust. I don't know if you knew that Virginia Woolf lived there for several years with her husband Leonard. If you like, we can visit it one day. I went with Martin a couple of years back. She suffered badly from depression and one day decided to drown herself in the Ouse – I think it was during the war – she filled her pockets...' Jenny stopped mid-sentence and looked across at Vanessa, who was smiling.

'Thank goodness I've got you and Martin. I'll treat you to this meal.'

40

'I feel that I've returned to the same situation with Vanessa that I was in a year ago.'

'Well, you'll just have to tell her, won't you? Like I said before, you can't keep meeting up with her so often.'

'In fact, it's worse now. I've finished my training, but I'm still new at the job and with Nicky so depressed at the moment, I have even less time to see her.'

'Let's rewind a bit here. Remember what I said, just tell her straight; she'll understand, she's your sister. She may be a bit upset, but she'll come round. It's not as if you're saying you're never going to see her again.'

'I can't, Martin.'

'Why on earth not? I don't understand. What are you afraid of? For goodness, sake, Jenny, she has her job and the twins and her daughter here.'

Jenny decided not to tell Martin about Jackie returning to Jo'burg. What was the point? They lay naked under the duvet as it had been frosty earlier in the day, and with cloud cover all morning, the bedroom hadn't warmed up. Once they had resurrected their physical relationship, they made a joint decision to leave one afternoon a week free and see what transpired. Some Monday afternoons, they just watched a DVD together on the sofa, but more often than not, their memory of earlier pleasures led them upstairs, with Jenny thinking that making a set time for lovemaking – she had read this in their Sunday paper's agony column – worked better than just waiting for a non-existent right time. Weekends were for family and trips out together. Weekdays were for work, volunteering, meeting up with Vanessa and sex. After lunch on a Monday, Jenny would go upstairs to their bedroom, switch on the oil-filled radiator, and with the anticipation increasing her arousal, she would then call down to Martin saying that the heating was on, while she undressed and inserted her pessary. He would then climb the stairs two at a time while loosening his clothes and join her under the duvet. He would go down on her until she begged him to stop, then she would take him into her mouth for barely a minute, until, panting, he would push her back on the bed and slide into her, ensuring their immediate climaxes. In the closeness that followed, Jenny felt she could raise matters she couldn't bring herself to say at any other time.

'Suppose I hadn't told you the truth about something?' she ventured as they lay under the duvet.

'Well, if it was in the past, it wouldn't matter, would it? Everyone has some things they don't want to tell their partner.'

Jenny thought, *he probably thinks that I'm trying to say I had an affair or have been attracted to someone else.* 'But what if it was important?'

'It couldn't be that important, or you would have told me, wouldn't you? Even if you had an abortion without telling me, it doesn't matter now. We decided years ago not to have a child. It's here and now that matters, not what you did or didn't do in the past. I think it's amazing that after all those years of research, you finally found your family. You meet up with the twins regularly, which you always look forward to, and you even found Vanessa. I know it's not always easy with her, but she's still your sister. Just tell her you can't see her so often and then invite her over here for a meal again.'

'When you put it like that it, sounds so simple.'

'Well, it is. It's not a problem, not for me, anyhow. You know I said before I couldn't do second rounds and thought I might need those little blue pills? Well, feel this.' He put her hand on his hardening penis and rolled on top of her. After rubbing himself between her breasts and against her stomach, he positioned himself between her legs and whispered, 'Shall we give it a try?'

*

Jenny chose the day carefully. The more she repeated Martin's words in her head, the more confident she became. *Just tell her straight; she won't refuse to see you. Then ask her over here for a meal.*

'This lunch is on me, Vanessa,' said Jenny as they entered the bar, the flames of the log fire that sat in the middle of the old brick fireplace warming them instantly. 'I do love the smell of burning logs, don't you?'

'Yes, me too. Look, it's my turn. You paid last week.'

'I know, but I've had a small lottery win, so it's my treat,' Jenny lied. 'Let's sit over there by the wall. I hate sitting in the middle of the room.'

'Well, seeing as you're paying, I'll have a starter then, I'm pretty hungry. Don't worry, I'm not having a sweet, not today anyway.' Vanessa grinned at her sister. 'This is cosy; we haven't been here before.'

'No, it's a bit further out, but worth it for the food. What do you fancy?' Jenny said, passing the lunch menu. 'The king prawns are good for a starter, that's what I'm going for.'

'Well, make that two then. You said you've been here before?'

'Yes, last year on Martin's birthday. What do you fancy to drink? I think I'll have a lager today. You usually have a white wine spritzer, is that OK?'

'Yes, that's fine.'

'Two king prawns, one white wine spritzer and a half of lager, please. Stella, if you have it, thank you. I don't know about you, but I can't stand to see both arms covered in tattoos. It doesn't look attractive on a woman, or a man for that matter,' Jenny whispered across the table as the waitress walked away. 'She's lovely without them.'

'It's just a fad. I do agree with you though. I don't mind tattoos, but just not covering all the skin. I've thought of having one done myself soon, something small, perhaps a protea flower, on the top of my leg perhaps, to surprise any future boyfriend and remind me of South Africa. I wanted to say, Jenny, I really appreciate you meeting up with me more often. I do realise you have less spare time than me, even though I work full-time. Also, I want you to know that I am thinking of what else I can do in the studying line, or perhaps changing my job.'

Jenny breathed deeply to calm her nerves. 'Thanks for saying that, Vanessa, but now you've mentioned it, I have been finding meeting up so often difficult. I was wondering if you could agree that we cut back on our meetings. Perhaps, once every two or three months instead of every week. Time goes so fast, what with my advice work and Nicky not doing so well again lately.'

'Not for me it doesn't, Jenny. Time, I mean, and as I said before, Nicky will have to manage on his own sometime, if and when you're not around.'

'Yes, I realise that, and of course I think about it. But while I am here, I need to support him when I can. Rob's still working full-time.'

'Is that why you offered to pay today, to butter me up?'

'What? No, of course not, Vanessa. We can still talk on the phone. It's just that meeting up so often has become too much for me.'

'So you would rather spend your time talking with strangers for nothing, than with your own sister who needs you?'

'It's not like that.'

'Yes, it is, if you didn't do that advice work, you would have more time for me.'

Jenny stared at Vanessa. She couldn't tell her that even if she didn't work as a volunteer, she still wouldn't want to meet up with her so often.

'I don't expect you've told the twins you can't meet up with them.'

'Well, no, but we don't meet up that often, so I don't need to.'

'But they have each other. They always have. I only

have you. I even moved down here so we could see more of each other.'

The tattooed waitress placed the starters in front of them, saying, 'I'll just bring your drinks over,' and walked back to the bar.

'I don't even see my daughter now,' Vanessa shouted, making the young couple at the next table stop eating to look around.

'Perhaps you could contact the twins again. We could meet them together then.' Jenny was searching for the right words to calm Vanessa but then realised that wasn't a good idea.

'Not after how they used to treat me, and what I told you. Cathy wouldn't meet with me anyway, so neither would Maddy.'

'Look, Vanessa, it's not about you, only my commitments.'

'Of course it's about me. If I remember, it was you who found me. I didn't ask you to, I never even knew you existed and now you don't want to know me. You with your perfect life with Martin. Does he know about this?'

'No, of course not, it's completely my decision. Also, my life isn't perfect, you know that, what with Nicky's mental health and Lorna's never been easy.'

'But, it's a damn site better than mine and you want to drop me just when I need you.'

'I'm not dropping you. I just don't want to meet up so often.'

'What's the difference?'

The tattooed barmaid had stopped wiping glasses and was staring at them from behind the bar, while the young couple had picked up their drinks and moved to another table.

'Look, Vanessa, let's just enjoy our meal.' Jenny picked up a prawn and snapped it, thinking she'd been right to worry. Why did she take any notice of what Martin said?

'Well, I won't enjoy mine.' Vanessa stood up, grabbed her coat from the back of her chair and strode towards the bar entrance. Jenny stared at the door as it slammed shut. The waitress returned.

'Are you OK? Have you decided on a mains?'

Jenny decided not to tell Martin what happened when she arrived home; she was upset and only mentioned where they had been and that they had enjoyed their lunch. The day after, she took a phone call from an ecstatic Maureen telling her that her daughter had contacted the intermediary to say she was ready now to meet her. She apologised for her earlier letter, saying that her mother had recently died, so that meeting her birth mother was the last thing she wanted to do at that time. Her adoptive father had discussed it with her recently, saying that he would support her when she was ready and suggested that it might be a good thing for her to do. Jenny was thrilled for Maureen, as she seldom knew the outcome of people's searches, and so was for a short time distracted from thinking about Vanessa. On the evening of the third day following their meeting, she dialled Vanessa's number. 'I've been wondering how you are, Vanessa. I'm sorry about the other day, if I upset you.'

'You've changed your mind, Jenny. I knew you would. So, we can meet up next week as usual and we'll forget the other day ever happened.'

Jenny drew a deep breath. 'No, I'm sorry, Vanessa, I can't. As I said, we can still meet up, but just not so often. I can't manage it.'

'Why are you phoning me then?'

'Well, to see how you are, of course, and to say I'm sorry you were upset.'

'But you're not, are you, sorry? If you were, we would carry on meeting as we have been. You know, Jenny, I've been thinking. You could be really sorry, if you know what I mean?'

Jenny's heart missed a beat and then quickened. 'What do you mean?' She gripped the edge of the windowsill.

'You know what I'm talking about.' Jenny's knuckles whitened as she gripped the sill harder. 'I could speak to Martin about what you said.'

'But he knows, Vanessa, he agreed with me that it would be best if I don't meet up with you so often. He would like to ask you over here for dinner soon,' Jenny said, thinking this would soften the blow.

'So, you have spoken to him about it. You said you hadn't. I can't bear the thought that the two of you have been talking about me and discussing about how often we should meet. That's so humiliating.'

'No, Vanessa, it was Martin who wanted you to come over for dinner. You can still come over here.' Jenny couldn't think of anything more to say as her fingers gripped the receiver to her ear.

'But he doesn't know everything, does he?'

Jenny stared out of the window at two men who were putting together a new wooden seat alongside the flint wall that surrounded the church.

'Did you hear what I said?'

'Yes,' she whispered.

'Think about it, Jenny. What's worse, meeting up with me once a week or so, as you should anyway to support me as your sister, or Martin knowing the truth?'

'But why would you tell him, Vanessa? I would never want to see you again if you did that. Would I?'

'You might; in fact, you probably would, when things go belly up once Martin knows who you really are. You can't think that wouldn't change things between you both? Once he knows he's been fucking his sister all these years. I don't think Maddy and Cathy would find that easy to forget either when I write to tell them about it. You're my sister, so we'd both be equally lonely then. I have nothing much to lose if you're only going to see me three or four times a year, and it's a no-brainer for you. Look, let's meet up next week as usual and we can forget we ever had this conversation. You decide where and I'll treat you to lunch this time. We can do that, surely?'

Jenny stepped back from the window reeling, her head spinning and her mouth suddenly dry. She had never heard Vanessa swear before. She was more shocked about that than the words she thought she had heard. 'OK. I'll call you at the beginning of next week.' Jenny slammed the receiver down on the handset and collapsed into the armchair in front of the window. *Did I really just have this conversation with Vanessa? It was surreal. Did I hear her right? Did she say and mean that she would tell Martin the truth about our relationship? Surely, she wouldn't do that? I must have imagined that was what she meant because I'm so sensitive about it. I'm reading far too much into her words. But what else would she tell Martin about? Perhaps she would just tell him that she was upset that I didn't want to see her so often, nothing else. But she said she would write to the twins, and she did say, 'He doesn't know everything, does he?' There's only one thing he doesn't know about and never can. Also, she said, 'You could be really sorry if you know what I mean?' and mentioned him knowing the truth. Did she actually say, 'Once he knows he's been fucking his sister all these years,' and how it would change things between us? Surely not. I've never heard her swear before. Oh God, I've been so stupid. Why did I ever tell her? I should never have told her, but sisters shouldn't have secrets from each other surely? She's right though. If we just carry on as we have been, everything will be fine. But how can I forgive Vanessa for what she just said she would do? But I wouldn't have to worry about Martin knowing anymore, or the twins.* Jenny recalled last Monday afternoon and how, because their sex life was now back on track, they were closer than ever. *If Martin did know, it would be the end of our life together, I am sure of that. No, I can't risk it, not after all this time. She's right. It is a no-brainer.*

41

'It's great to see you again, Jenny. It's been quite a while,' said Maddy.

'Yes, where have you been all these months?' added Cathy.

'I know, it's been too long, but I've had a lot going on,' Jenny said, thinking that neither of them had bothered to phone her to find out why she hadn't been in touch. She remembered Vanessa's words about them not needing anyone else. They sank into the new velvet armchairs now provided by the café.

'These are so comfy; we won't want to leave, will we? Lucky you, tell us all about it. "A lot going on" has sexual overtones in my book.' Cathy smiled, her eyes crinkling at the corners. 'Are you and Martin good, or is there someone else on the scene? Tell us all.'

'Martin and I are fine; in fact, we're more than fine. Also, I've been accepted as an advisor at Citizens Advice. I think I mentioned I was applying last time we met, so I've had to do their training, but that's over now. But it's been a bit difficult lately with Vanessa.'

'Ah, I knew it. Vanessa's been up to her old tricks

again. You know what I mean? Maddy told you what she did to me and Gerrit. You make sure she's not alone with Martin.'

'Yes, I will, don't worry.' Jenny smiled, thinking that Cathy's remark struck home, but that was the least of her worries. 'She's given up her OU degree course, saying it's all too difficult and she can't cope, so I've been supporting her more than before. Martin helped her a lot with the formulas and wording, but she still said she was giving up.'

'I think I told you she wasn't academic,' Maddy added. 'But, that's a shame for her. She probably rushed into it without thinking it through properly. You know, the amount of work and time it would involve for her. That's Vanessa though, very unpredictable and impulsive at times, but she can be really sweet.'

'Only when things are going her way,' said Cathy.

Jenny thought back to the newspaper article but said nothing.

'She's not like us; in fact, you're not to breathe a word, but we're not really sure she's actually our sister.'

'What do you mean?' Jenny felt blood draining from her face as she leaned forward in her chair to be sure she heard Maddy correctly.

'Well, she's definitely our half-sister. But rumours were going around when we were young. One afternoon, we overheard Dad's sisters talking together when they were alone. They came to visit us – we hardly ever saw any relatives, so that was quite an occasion – they were saying that our mother was a trollop and was having an affair – we remembered the word – trollop – because it sounds

211

so funny and we had to look it up in the dictionary. We didn't know what an affair was back then. That would have been around the time Vanessa was conceived or a couple of years after. There was a lot of talk about a man at her church – she was very religious, our mother – he was always coming to our house, church business we were told. Of course, we don't know for sure as our parents remained married, but we've always had our suspicions, haven't we, Cathy?'

'Yes, we have.' Cathy nodded.

'So, if you're right, she's not even my half-sister. We're not related at all?' Jenny exclaimed, her heart jumping around in her chest.

'But we can't be sure, Jenny, it's just what we overheard and she's so different from us in lots of ways. But we never let it affect our relationship with her when we were growing up, did we, Cathy? Of course, it was different after what she did to Cathy and Gerrit. But you don't have any reason not to carry on seeing her. But, for God's sake, don't breathe a word of what we've just said, as we're not sure that she knows anything about it. She can still tell you a lot about our life and family in South Africa. Just keep her away from Martin,' she added.

Little do they know, thought Jenny. That she has a very good reason to carry on seeing Vanessa. She remembered Vanessa saying that she had never felt included by the twins as a child, but that may have had nothing to do with her parentage, it was probably just because they were twins and the age gap between them.

'Look, I think you need cheering up. Come over next Sunday for lunch, all the family will be there and Cathy's children. It's not often that happens. You can tell us more about your advice work and don't forget to bring Martin this time. He can't still be doing his surveying in this weather. I'm going to get us some more coffee or we'll be told to leave. Flat white, Jenny?'

'Talking of Martin,' said Cathy, once Maddy had left. 'What did you mean when you said that things are more than fine between you both? I sense some erotic activity, so come on, spill the beans, I could do with some sexy tips. Remember, no secrets between sisters.'

42

Jenny recognised Gail by her blue, spiky hair as she crossed the south coast road towards Hove Lagoon. Gail was seated on the wall and held a brindle French bulldog on a lead. 'So, you did dye your hair then? You said you were going to the last time we met,' she said as she approached her friend and gave her a hug. 'I love the matching earrings too.'

'Yes, I'm keeping it blue for a year to raise money for charity,' Gail said as she stood up and hugged her friend.

'What one's that?'

'Brighton Housing Trust. I had a lot of dealings with the charity when I was a councillor.'

'Yes, housing is such an important issue. We are always having queries about the lack of suitable accommodation at Citizens Advice. I'll give you a contribution when I get home.'

'It's good that you're enjoying the work there. So, how's life treating you then, Jenny?' Gail asked as they wandered passed the lagoon towards the sea. 'I was so happy for you when you told me you had found your family after all those years. I think that's amazing. Go on then, Annie.' Gail bent down to let her dog of the lead. 'This one's so different to Sadie. You wouldn't believe how two dogs of the same breed can be so different.'

'Shall we walk along to Matteo's as usual? It's such a sunny day for so early in the year.'

'I must say, you don't look as happy as you did last year when we met. Isn't the long wished-for family reunion going well?'

'It is with the twins, Maddy and Cathy. We meet up regularly, visit each other's houses and they've told me so much about their lives when they were younger before they came to England. But with both of my brothers living so far away, we only keep in touch by e-mail. But we plan to go and see Alastair in France later this year.'

'Go on, Annie, have a run. She's never keen to leave my side. She's still quite nervous, not like Sadie,' Gail said as she bent down to stroke and urge the dog forward. 'Isn't there another sister who moved down this way?'

'Yes, Vanessa, she lives in Bexhill.'

'You still see her too?'

'Yes.'

'Do I detect a "but" coming?'

'No, look, Gail, just forget about my family for a moment. I want to run something past you. A friend at my book group has asked me for some advice, as she thinks she's being emotionally blackmailed.'

Gail immediately turned to look at Jenny and frowned. 'Really? Go on then.'

'Well, she said to me that she told a woman who she thought was a friend a secret, which she should never have told her, because if it were known, it would be so damaging, especially if her husband knew about it. Don't look at me like that, Gail. I just need to run this past you to see what you think.'

'Carry on then. Do you mean this so-called friend of hers has threatened to tell her husband this secret?'

'Yes, and if she did that, it would mean the end of their marriage.'

'But, why on earth did she tell her friend the secret in the first place? And why would a friend do that?'

'She said that, about a year ago, they were in a pub one evening confiding in each other, well, moaning about their marriages, to be exact, and my friend had too much to drink and let slip her secret. But then recently, she – my friend – decided that she doesn't want to see this woman anymore because she has a drink problem – the friend, that is – or not to cut off contact completely, but not see her so often. So she told her friend it was becoming too much for her meeting up each week, as she has problems of her own and was finding it difficult to cope with those. But her friend didn't accept the situation and started shouting at her, saying, she's going through a really difficult time, and that she – my friend – is helping her by meeting up regularly and she needs her support. She then intimated, well, more than that really, she threatened to tell my friend's husband her secret, and that he would be shocked if he knew about it. So, I wondered what you would say. I've been going over and over about what to say to her in my mind.'

'Well, firstly, your friend shouldn't meet up with her in a pub, bad idea. Then I would advise your friend to call her bluff, not to give in to emotional blackmail. Her friend probably wouldn't actually tell her husband this secret anyway. She's just saying that because she's so upset. Your friend could suggest counselling or AA, there's plenty of help and support out there. Also, why doesn't your friend tell her husband this secret herself? What on earth can be that bad? It probably wouldn't mean the end of her marriage anyway. Did she have an affair?'

Jenny thought and, just for a moment, wondered whether to tell Gail the truth, but decided no, she couldn't; it would be too complicated and devastating. 'Yes, she did have an affair and she had to have an abortion,' Jenny said, trying to make the secret as damaging as she could.

'OK, well, as I see it, she has two choices, your friend. Either come clean to her husband herself, so then she has nothing further to fear from her friend, but then there's the risk he'll never forgive her and her marriage could be over. Or, if not over, never the same. Or else say nothing and carry on seeing her friend. But supposing it escalates and her friend starts asking for money – it could if she has a drink problem – you know, proper blackmail. People with addictions always lie and steal to feed them. If that happens, then she should go to the police. From the years I spent as a councillor, I've always found the police very helpful. Remember that blackmailers are almost always the weaker party, so your friend should be strong, call her bluff and not give into her. Look, let's sit on that empty seat, I could do with a sit down and we can enjoy watching the sea; those waves are crashing in today.'

The friends sat in silence for a while with Annie fussing around Gail's legs. 'I was so lonely when Jerry died, especially at the weekends, so I bought Annie from a dog rescue centre. I think she must have had a bad experience before she came to me, because she's still very nervous. But walking a dog has been good therapy for me. I chat to and get to know so many people down here.'

Jenny leaned down and stroked Annie. 'Thank you for your thoughts, Gail. I was thinking along the same lines myself. I'll let my friend know that I think she should call her bluff.'

'Look, Jenny, I've known you for years, you're my oldest and best friend. I can see from your face that you're worried about something serious, and it doesn't take Albert Einstein to work out it's something to do with what we've been talking about. I'm not convinced you've told me the truth. You and Martin seem so good together that I'm sure both of you could cope with any secret that either of you have, even an affair and an abortion. But that's all you've told me, so that's my advice. I won't press you to tell me what the problem is. If it's anything different from what you said, I can't think what an earth it could be that you aren't able to tell me and Martin. So, I'll leave it at that. What I will say, though, is that if it's anything you've done that's broken the law, my advice is for you to come clean and go to the police.'

Jenny knew she had broken the law but had always rationalised it by saying to herself that because she hadn't known of their blood relationship when they decided to live together, and, also, because they were adults, it was somehow a lesser crime. Also, Martin had broken the law too, but he wasn't aware that he had. Was that a defence? Don't they say that ignorance is no defence? They hadn't married, or had a child together, she had made sure of both of those. She couldn't imagine presenting herself at Brighton Police Station to admit to incest, whatever Gail advised. Would she be charged? Would it be in the newspapers – local and national – everyone would know; Lorna, Nicky and Daniel and her new family as well. That was just too terrible to contemplate. 'Thank you, Gail, you're a true friend. Let's carry on walking, shall we? The ice creams are my treat today.'

'I'm so pleased that everything is going so well with your new family. I think it's fantastic that you managed to find them and that they're here in England. Well, your sisters at least, that's a miracle.'

Jenny smiled and nodded at her friend as she rose from the seat.

43

Jenny parked in the road that forked into two and surrounded the windmill, leaving it isolated on its patch of green. She pulled the hood on her coat over her head and walked over to the church in the drizzle. She remembered it had been drizzling that day in November when she had met Martin again. He had been laying flowers on his mother's grave, as it had been the third anniversary of her death. She hadn't seen him there until he had walked over to her. She thought now, for the first time, that if her parents hadn't died in the October of that year, she would never have been at the churchyard that day and so would never have met Martin again. At some time after her parents had died, she was sure that she would have wanted to know the identity of her birth mother and possibly trace her. She would then have been shocked to find out that, years before, she had gone out with Martin, but that would have been the end of the matter.

She opened the gate to the churchyard and stood in front of her parents' grave. She remembered her mother's words to her as a child, 'never tell lies, Jenny, they'll always find out.' She had lied in the past, but only because of her situation and because she had been unable to admit the truth to anyone. She had certainly lied to Martin by omission, knowing he could never discover the truth. Perhaps she should have told him as soon as she had seen her original birth certificate that revealed the name of her birth mother, when, not believing it to be true, she had ordered the birth certificates of Martin and Anna, which then confirmed their mother as her own. She had certainly been in shock, as he would have been if she had told him then. But they had given up so much to be together, they might have been able to have buried it, like an older relative who had died and, afterwards, was only remembered occasionally. If she told him now, how could he forgive her for hiding something so important? *I even denied him the chance of another child that I knew he wanted and could possibly have had with Marilyn, or somebody else, and a second marriage. No, it's impossible now.* After spending ten minutes pulling out the weeds that had multiplied around the edge of the grave, she stood up, brushed the mud from the bottom of her jeans and walked the few yards to the grave of Martin's mother and father. She didn't linger. *He hardly ever comes here now*, she thought. She would remind him later, and he could come over on his own. She made sure they never came here together – that would be too much – so she always made an excuse. She looked up at the wooden sails on the windmill and thought, *all my childhood was spent in sight of them, but it was a happy time; now I'm in their shadow.*

Deciding not to drive home straight away, Jenny wandered across the main road that in the 1930s had replaced the ancient track that had linked West Blatchington with the hamlet of Hangleton. She stood outside the upstairs flat where her parents had lived for nearly forty years and walked up the short path and opened the side gate, passing the front door of their old neighbour's downstairs flat. She stood and stared at the large, concreted area. No sign of what had been a large rockery filled with colourful plants, or the climbing white rose that had been tethered against the brick wall. A few large, rusty nails protruded from the cement pointing. No evidence either that a lawn had once lain next to the rockery, edged by a trellis covered by a red climbing rose. They had been her father's favourite flowers. Behind that had been a small, triangular vegetable garden. Now just a gnarled apple tree standing in a metre square of earth remained. She turned and walked back through the gate. The front garden, like the majority in the road, had also been concreted over. Instead of a lawn surrounded by flower borders, there was now a car-standing area. Just a few lonely sprigs of blue aubretia emerged from the one remaining brick container that, with its twin, had guarded the path to their front door. She took a deep breath and smelt again the perfume of the night-scented stocks that had flowered in the border every summer. Stepping onto the pavement, she turned right, noticing that the flat next door had cardboard instead of glass inserted in the downstairs window. She walked to the corner of the road, where each summer she would sit with Gail on a grassy bank overlooking wheat fields that stretched to the Dyke. The fields had now disappeared, along with the house martins that used to nest under the eaves of the houses.

Overgrown scrubland – growing taller each year – now replaced the fields as the area waited for the approval of a planned development of eight hundred houses, a school and a parade of shops. Turning the corner, she wandered up the hill, noticing that the cash-strapped council had replaced many of the original square paving slabs – ideal for hopscotch – with tarmac to a row of shops that years before had served the daily needs of the whole community, including gossiping. Today, there was no one else about and only an all-day convenience store and a chemist were open; the others remained shuttered. *Changing times*, thought Jenny, *but not always for the better. Time to go.*

'There you are. I've been wondering where you were.' She heard Martin's words as she slammed the front door behind her. 'I didn't think you would be going out this afternoon, in this weather, it's not very springlike. I've put one of those chicken pies that we like in the oven, but it won't be ready for another half hour.'

'I hadn't planned to go out. I just needed some time away on my own to think about things. I'll lay the table. By the way, I've decided to leave Citizens Advice.'

'No, surely not, you really enjoy working there, and it wasn't long ago you completed the training. Also, it gets you out of my hair for one day a week.' Martin grinned.

'You're right, I do enjoy it, so I'm hoping I can get back to it later when I have more time and when Nicky's more stable.'

'But he has been lately, Jenn. You said the other day how different he's been since he met that girl from his support group. Sarah, isn't it? You haven't had to phone

223

him or go over there nearly so often and you've looked so much more relaxed; well, you did until the other day. If you didn't see so much of Vanessa, that would help. I can't understand why you still haven't told her that you need to cut back on the days you meet up, especially after you've been going on about it so much.'

'Well, it's still early days with Sarah. Remember how depressed he became and how worried I was when his previous relationship ended? Anyway, it's fine about Vanessa, Martin. I enjoy seeing her and we've become quite close lately. Look, I'll get the veggies out and pour us a juice. We must be serious about cutting back on the alcohol. We keep saying we will, but we never do, so that changes from today,' Jenny said, noticing for the first time how sparse his hair had become. *Just like Ricco's used to be*, she thought.

'By the way, speaking of Vanessa, she phoned twice while you were out. So I said you would call her back. If you want me to, I could speak to her about you not meeting up so often. She might accept it better from me.'

'No, please don't ever do that, Martin. As I said, we've become quite close lately. I can deal with it.'

He turned and stared at her. 'OK, it was just a suggestion.'

'You need to go and check on your parents' grave. I was thinking that when I drove past the church the other day. It's been a long time since you went there. It must be covered in weeds by now after all the rain we've had.' Jenny walked over and stared out of the kitchen window through the drizzle at the holly tree, now denuded of its scarlet berries by a winter flock of redwings.

'Jenny, did you hear what I said about Vanessa? She called twice.'

'Yes, I heard you. I'll call her back, but not just now. Let's eat first.'

About the Author

Following a career in Accountancy, Tricia studied Creative Writing at Sussex University and wrote her first novel *Unwanted Truths*. She has two daughters and lives in Brighton with her husband and Luca the family cat.